Visit the author's website at www.adamfoxauthor.co.uk[2]

Published by Foxes' Retreat Ltd, Ashbourne, United Kingdom.

Visit the publisher's website at www.foxesretreat.com[3]

Book Cover by Adam Fox and Zain Ali

Editing by Manda Waller www.mandawaller.co.uk[4]

1st edition 2023

ISBN (print) 978-1-7384340-0-8

ISBN (e-book) 978-1-7384340-1-5

---

1. http://www.foxesretreat.com

2. http://www.adamfoxauthor.co.uk

3. http://www.foxesretreat.com

4. http://www.mandawaller.co.uk

Dedicated to Ailesh McCaffrey,
hydrophobic traveller dog extraordinaire.

Vardo Witch
A Vardo Novella, Kurra's Story
by Adam Fox

Chapter 1

"For what didst thou call me, pillock?" Kurra's voice was low and harsh, her anger palpable.

"I didn't know you'd be real, did I?" The boy looked shaken, the saucer of milk spilling where he held it, tipping, in trembling fingers.

"That's charmin', that is. Real. Thou wouldn't know real if it hit thee in thy face." The hobgoblin pulled herself up to her full height, and looked up at the boy, who was as tall again, even though he was ... what? She looked at him with more attention. Nine years old? Ten? "I've been asleep for 'undreds of years an' thou brings me back to the breathin' world, for this?" She waved her overlarge hand at the mill's dusty floor.

"I'm right sorry, like. Didn't know you were asleep." The boy looked like he would cry at any moment.

"An' don't spill the milk, neither! Give it 'ere." She took the saucer and tipped it up into her mouth, drinking the milk down with a loud slurp. "Ah. Better." She wiped her lips with the back of her large, hairy hand. "Now then. As I'm 'ere, I best get workin'. I'll see this cleaned. What's thy name?"

The boy was staring at her with eyes so wide they looked like they might pop out of their sockets.

"J-Joseph," he stammered. "Joseph Foden."

"An' I'm Kurra. Or thou may call me hob, Joseph-sire."

"Wh-what do I do now?"

"Well, sire. Whatever it is thou wish. You're my kyrios, my master. I will clean and polish. I will be in this room, or nearby; if thou needs me, call my name."

Kurra looked around the room, then. Row upon row of machines lined the wall, great loops of threads strung over the space. Serried ranks of cotton bobbins, hundreds of them, ranged on frames into the distant reaches of the vast space. White fluffy bundles of cotton were piled on the dusty wooden planked floor under the machines. Dust and cobwebs clung to the low ceiling beams. A layer of grime covered the high windows, weakening the golden, slanted light of the evening. The machines were silent, inactive.

"Y-you have to clean ... under the mules ..." Joseph began, gesturing to a pile of empty sacks by the wall, brushes and dustpans hanging on hooks.

"That's not the only place as needs a cleanin'," Kurra retorted, sweeping her gaze over the machines, the windows. "Might take me a few days." She saw the lad's panicked face. "I'll clean under the mules first, though. Don't fret."

She pressed into the other part of space and time, the slow part, and stepped through. Her huge hands set to cleaning, sweeping up the piles of cotton, pushing them into a hessian sack that was soon bulging. She worked from one end of the spinning mules to the other, keeping a diligent eye on the lad as he stood, frozen in time, the dust motes stationary in the oblique light. She used a small brush to clean the threads and the frames and the trays, the spindles and the shuttles and the winders. Five sacks filled. She paused. The boy had turned his head a half towards her. She released the pressure on space-time, stepped back to the present, and the world sped up.

"There thou art. I'll see to the windows an' suchlike in the followin' days. Be there a space I can settle into? A quiet space, mind. I imagine this 'ere room is right noisy in the day?" She looked up at Joseph, whose mouth was opening and closing, speechless, his face a mask of wonder. She smiled. From his point of view, she had cleaned the cotton up in the time it took to turn his head. "Don't go tellin' thy mates thou hast an 'elper or they'll all want one."

"That's ... um ... how?" squeaked Joseph.

"I'm a hob. A quiet space? Sire?"

"Y-yes, of course. Up here. Follow me." He walked over to a ladder on the far wall that was set against a hatch in the roof space. He climbed; Kurra followed. The hatch let into a loft, crowded with old boxes and broken machinery. The backs of the roof tiles were visible in the ceiling's slope above, everything dusty and dim lit through a filthy skylight set into the tiles. "Will this be sufficient?" he asked.

"Aye, thank thee. I shall see thee tomorrow eve if thou wishes?" Kurra felt uncomfortable asking, but Avennio Cavarum was still fresh in her memory. A shiver ran down her spine. Best to set out her requirements. The lad looked so wet behind the ears he would more than likely forget, otherwise. "I don't wish to speak out of place, sire, but another bowl of milk would be a grand thing for me on the morrow?" She realised she was wringing her hands, ingratiating herself. Embarrassing.

"Oh! Yes, of course." Joseph bobbed his head. "I'd best get off, or'se I'll miss dinner." He almost ran from the loft space, slipping out and down the ladder in a sudden hurry.

Kurra looked around her.

"Well, Kurra, lass," she muttered. "Thine kyrios seems pleasant enough. But thou hast best get this room cleaned an' all, if it be thine abode."

THE FOLLOWING MORNING, the tolling of the factory bell woke Kurra at six, as it called the workers to start their day. The bell's location in the tower above her loft made it resonate with a powerful and deafening sound. Despite stuffing her ears with cotton, she could not get back to sleep.

"I reckon there might be summat wrong with the bell, on the morrow," she muttered as she entertained thoughts of stealing the clapper, or the rope, or gumming up whatever mechanism caused the tolling. She stretched on her pallet bed, looked around; she had pushed boxes together, pulled a sheet of cloth over a line stretched between beams. Her quarters were comfortable, private, her bed warm enough. "Best night's sleep I've 'ad in a while, that. Notwithstanding the rude awakenin'. Joseph best bring the milk, mind."

She rolled out of bed, padded over to the box that was doubling as a table.

"I must 'ave been tired as a dog last night, I didn't put thy shrine up, My Lady." She closed her eyes and reached into the between place, her place, and pulled back the stub of a candle and a tiny effigy of Hestia, goddess of the hearth. The figure had a waxy texture, with red hair cascading down its back, and wore white robes crafted from muslin cloth. She set the effigy and the stub of the candle on a packing box and incanted the fire spell in a language she didn't understand. She had memorised the word sounds ... when? So long ago, it predated her earliest memory.

The candle sputtered into flame, and she offered a prayer.

"Hestia, guardian of the hearth's gentle glow, grant me luck and safety where're I may go. Give me strength to tarry here. May my service last a year." She smiled. As if Hestia were listening. She didn't know if anyone worshipped the Old Gods anymore. The Christians seemed to be everywhere. At least in Europa. She daydreamed for a while, watching the candle burn down. Thought back to her meeting with Hestia, made corporeal, so many years ago. The goddess had come to her aid, with her flaming red hair and her fiery red eyes. She was glad to have met her, and continued to worship her, giving thanks to her support every day.

Noises filtered up from the workroom below. Voices. Men, women, children. The thrum of the belt drives starting up, some immense machinery driven by a waterwheel churning, pushing. She could feel it in the brickwork's vibration. As if the entire building was waking up, stretching and yawning like a colossal brick-built dog.

She snuffed the candle out and climbed through a gap in the boxes to a section of the floor that didn't have planks; it gave her a clear view of the room below, the spinning mules, the workers filing in. Joseph searched the area for her arrival. Well, he'd have to call her if he wanted her. He could see her, but no one else would unless they had the sight. She mused on this as she sat with her legs dangling. The gift, some called it. Though it sent some mad. Not such a gift when you see things that others can't.

WATCHING FROM HER VANTAGE point, she considered the workers, the machines. The mules, spinning flaxen cotton and wool into yarn, rumbled and clattered, filling the room with an almost tangible wall of noise. Joseph and another child scampered under the weft of the machines, inside the mules, sweeping the dropped cotton from the floor, dragging hessian sacks after them. They were nimble, crawling in the space under the machine as it expanded, then scooting back as the machine retracted. To Kurra's eye, it looked like difficult, dangerous work for a child.

The men operating the machines tended the cotton bobbins, reattaching threads when they snapped, oiling the spindles as they worked. A fine mist of machine oil, flung from the spindles, lingered in the air. It caught in Kurra's throat. What it must be like down there, with the cotton dust and fibres, and the mist of oil? She was at once thankful that she didn't have to work amongst the machines whilst they ran and fearful for Joseph's safety and health. With chagrin, she thought of the other child, a girl of perhaps seven years. She, too, would be breathing in all sorts of noxious material.

As she sat and watched, her mind wandered. She thought of her long years of servitude, and her longer years of hibernation. The world was changing. With each return, industry and iron grew. Fewer of her own species. Fewer of all the fae. She hadn't seen an elf in a hundred years. The last of her own kind she had met, Kamila, was whilst in the service of an abbot in a monastery, some four hundred years earlier.

Were they all dead? Or stuck between the worlds, as this world's iron sapped the magic? Or had they reached nirvana, the fabled Khôra, that place between worlds?

Khôra had been called a haven for the fae; rumoured to be controlled by the Tuatha de Danann, the elves of Eireann. She wasn't even sure that Khôra existed – it sounded too good to be true. But if it did, it might be a place she should think about making her way towards.

"I BRUNG YOU THE MILK, like." Joseph set a corked bottle down on the table – an upturned packing crate with a cloth over it – and smiled at Kurra, his grin toothy, his brown hair flopping lank to one side.

"Thank thee, sire. It is welcome." She had swept as she had yesterday, once the men had departed, and Joseph had persuaded his friend from the workhouse to leave. The girl was glad to give her work to Joseph, but Kurra noticed a fear in her as if she doubted the gift was without strings. Of course, the girl didn't know that Joseph would need to do little to have the floor, the windows, the machines spotless. Kurra was comfortable with this arrangement since she got a bottle of milk out of it. A bottle! She felt a warming glow of anticipation in her stomach.

"Thy job has the look of danger about it, sweepin' whilst the machines be runnin'?" she asked, eyeing the bottle and wondering how soon Joseph would leave.

"Aye, it's best to keep your head down when you're under the mule. When I'm twelve, I'll get to apprentice to Harold, and he'll show me how to spin the thread. Then I'll not have to skip under the machines so much."

"Well. I hope thou always remembers to keep thy 'ead down."

"You don't have to worry about me. I'm quick." He flashed that lopsided smile again. Kurra did worry about him. And not just because he brought bottles of milk. She'd offer a prayer for his continued safety, tonight, when she propitiated Hestia.

EVERY MORNING, THE bell tolled. Every morning, Kurra muttered and groaned in her cot, thoughts of clapper destruction and bell-rope cutting uppermost in her mind.

Every day, she prayed to Hestia, with the dwindling hope of ever hearing an answer. Were hearths not everywhere? The goddess of the hearth should still be in people's lives. But no.

Every day, she watched the men work and the children sweep. The supervisor would come by and observe, ensuring all was in order.

Every evening, she cleaned and swept and polished and dusted. This mule-spinning room had become renowned in the factory as the best-kept and cleanest. Joseph was proud, which made Kurra proud.

Every evening, Joseph brought her a bottle of milk, always fresh, always welcome.

Every Sunday, the mill was quiet and empty, and Kurra missed the noise and the bustle. And the milk. It was but one day in seven, and she knew Joseph would come on the morrow.

The routine of the days, the weeks, brought solace to her, and she forgot she was – as far as she could tell – alone in the world, in terms of her kin, or of other fae. She was content, and reasonably busy when she needed to be busy, and able to spend most of her days in quiet contemplation.

THE BELL TOLLED. ITS timbre was off, to Kurra's ears. As if it were cracked, or somehow otherwise dissonant. Discordant. Bells had their own magic, poured into the mould at the foundry by the bell smiths who pulled the spark of the bell from the ether. She didn't begin to understand it but found herself out of sorts at being woken by the jarring ring of it. Lying awake in her cot, she watched the rain sheeting onto the skylight set in the roof above. Her breath misted in the frigid air. Autumn must be on the way. She hadn't been outside for all of the summer of this work at the mill.

"I'd best get up, though," she muttered. The workers were arriving, and she felt the pull of the waterwheel as it engaged with the day's work, the rumble and tremor running through the fabric of the building.

She offered a morning prayer to Hestia, whilst regarding the desultory stub of the candle. She'd need to get another from somewhere. Maybe Joseph could get one for her?

As the morning progressed, she took up her accustomed seat overlooking the room that housed the spinning mules. Joseph and the girl were busy as usual, scooting under the whirring machinery, leaping back just in time as the ponderous frames extended and retracted over the floor.

The door to the room crashed open and the mill owner, Arkwright, all beard and fob chain and straining waistcoat, thundered into the room. A tall, spider-like man in a black cloak and stove-pipe top hat accompanied him. Their expressions were severe, grim.

"Harold Smith! You're wanted by the magistrates!" Arkwright shouted over the clamour of the room, spittle flecking his lips. Not just Harold, working at the spindles, but everyone in the room stopped to stare. Kurra watched, but she watched Joseph, a prickle of fear tingling at the nape of her neck. The girl ducked down. But Joseph gawped from just below the loom of the cotton lines. He seemed oblivious to the approaching frame end, rumbling on its wheels over the floorboards as the belt-powered mechanism pulled it inwards with inevitability.

From the water rushing along the millrace, piling against the wheel, driving the gigantic cogs, and reaching this room through a series of shafts and pulleys, the mechanism had power and strength. Kurra could feel it. She reached into slow time, freezing the movement, and leapt up, ran to the ladder, panic filling her. She stumbled at the top. In her hurry to reach Joseph, she missed her footing. Tripped and off balance, she fell through the loft hatch, clawing in desperation towards the rungs of the ladder. They whisked past, scant inches beyond her fingertips.

She landed on the ground with a thump that emptied her lungs. Her vision swam and wavered. She shook herself down, heaved in a breath of air. Then realised she was no longer in the slow space, but back in real time. With fear reaching into her soul like a terrible icy claw, she mashed down on her slow time again and rushed to the spinning mule, and Joseph.

For Kurra, time had all but stopped, so she had ample of it to take in the diorama frozen before her. Arkwright and the black-cloaked bailiff were glaring at Harold, who wore a look of abject fear and was facing them from the front of the machine. The girl was looking at Joseph, hands outstretched in supplication or alarm, her nascent scream forming but not yet leaving her throat. And Joseph. Oh, Joseph. Kurra was too late. Even though time was nearly stopped, he was already dead. Even though he was crouched, still upright, the roller beam had caught him fast against the back of the machine's carriage frame. His skull was the wrong shape, and crimson blood was just leaking from the rips showing in his skin, from his ears, his eyes.

Unable to bear to watch, Kurra spun around and rushed back to the ladder, hurling herself up in fury and self-loathing, in despair and grief. Joseph. He had been kind, full of life, full of hope.

She stepped back into time, letting the noise of the machinery, the child's scream, the shouts from the men wash over her. She flung herself face down on the bed. As the power from Joseph's spell faded, as his life faded, she could feel the pull of the between place. She looked over at her shrine to Hestia.

"Thou canst not expect duty an' devotion from thine acolytes if thou canst not keep mine kyrios alive for more than a season," she spat. She gathered up the figurine of the goddess and flung it at the far wall. Picked up the candle stub and went to fling that too, but thought better of it and, reaching through the veil, placed it in her place. You never knew when you'd need a candle. 'Hestia, though, I'm done with thee," she declared to the walls.

As had happened so many times before, without a kyrios to anchor her, she felt unutterably tired. She fell back onto her cot, almost unable to arrange her limbs before she slipped into somnolence and faded, once more, from the world of men.

Chapter 2

Kurra woke to heat and noise as if she had been transported from her slumber into the depths of Tartarus. She whimpered and shielded her eyes from the intense temperature.

"Here you are. Drink up." A rough voice, rough hands. A bowl of milk was thrust into her face, her mouth. She spat and tried to turn her head, but gnarled, strong, calloused hands held the back of her head, forcing her to drink. Most of the white liquid spilt down her front but some made it into her mouth. She gagged. Opened her eyes, squinting against the strong light, the incandescence. The fierce blast was coming from a roaring fire, so intense and bright it felt like it was burning her eyes. Her skin prickled with sweat and fear.

"Get to work then, 'ob. I need that coal shovelin' in that 'ole there. Quick now." The man let her go with a suddenness that made her stagger backwards. She bumped against a brick wall and looked around again, now she was slightly further from the turbulent furnace. She was in a smoky, sooty, rounded building, all old red brick and high distant curved ceilings. A pile of blackened hessian sacks rested to one side. The furnace, or whatever it was, sat like a giant's bottle made from bricks, in the centre of the room, stretching up and through the darkened roof high above. There was a shovel next to the sacks. One sack was split open, the lustrous coal tumbling onto the black dust floor.

"I'm a hob. I clean, I don't shovel!" she remonstrated with the wiry, weasel-faced man. He looked at her with, she realised, a face filled with hatred.

"Fuckin' shovel or'se I'll lam yer one with it. You cost me plenty to get brought 'ere." He paused, rubbing his heavily tattooed forearm. "And by Christ, you'll fuckin' work or'se it will go badly for yer." He cuffed her around the head, and her vision danced with sparks and lights. She fell onto all fours, and he kicked her in the chest, lifting her off the ground. She crashed down onto the sacks of coal; felt something break, or bruise, on her back. Pain speared through her. She cried out, stifled it as much as she could. Rolled. She had landed on the edge of the shovel.

"Get to work, whore!" he raged, standing over her. He went to kick her again, and she scrambled to her feet, scattering chunks of coal, putting some distance between them. She grabbed the shovel and did as she was ordered, shaking her head all the while, trying to clear her vision.

The heat was monumental. The shovel was huge. She was strong, but her back was bruised, her side ached. The milk had been off, as well. Yet still, she was bound, beyond her comprehension, to a vile example of humanity. Oh, this was looking bad. Avennio Cavarum was a dance in the glade compared to this.

KURRA SHOVELLED COAL for three days, without cease. On the third day, with the kiln nearing the end of its burn, her master stopped working and started drinking beer, sitting on a stool at the entrance to the furnace building.

She approached him with caution, ready to duck away if he became enraged or threw a punch for the fun of it.

"I wonder, sire, if sire has some milk, p'raps? I haven't had a drink in days an' I be right parched."

"You little shit. Do you think I 'ave milk? Here, fetch water from the tap if you're thirsty." He waved out into the yard abutting the kiln building, where a standpipe dripped water. She hurried to it and slaked her thirst, though the tap's flow was weak and the water brackish.

Over the next few days, she considered her luck. Or lack of it. Her new kyrios was named John Francis, and he was possibly worse than the Pope's housekeeper in Avennio Cavarum who had worked Kurra constantly and spared her very little in the way of milk. John was equitable with the milk when he remembered, but also with his fists and boots. Especially when he had taken a drink. Which was all the time.

Often, he would rage at her for little or no reason she could glean, spittle flying from his mouth as he emitted a torrent of verbal vitriol over her.

After the firing of the kiln was done, she was put to work cleaning the area around it, and the yard outside. For the first time in longer than she could remember, she was able to properly step outside. But the sky was soot black with smoke, the air thick with dust and poisonous vapour, and the ground underfoot grey and rocky. Nothing green or blue showed, as if the earth itself had died.

She had no quiet place to call her own, no cot, no space in which to rest.

"Make yersen hid, when the men are here, or'se I'll lam yer!" were her instructions when the potters came to collect the fired stoneware that was ensconced in the enormous saggers which were stacked inside the kiln, almost to the roof line. And hide she did, in the darker corners of the building, sometimes in the between place, though it was cold.

Then the kiln was ready to fire again, and she was back to work, shovelling coal and dancing out of the way of John's drunken swipes and kicks.

AFTER THREE KILN FIRINGS, over two weeks of daily abuse, physical assault and hot, sweaty, back-breaking work with meagre soured milk or brackish water from the standpipe to slake her thirst, Kurra had had enough. Something snapped inside her, and thoughts of doing harm to John darkened her mind. It wasn't the hob way; it was well outside the hob lore to even consider one's kyrios in a negative light. But, thought Kurra, enough was enough. The lore could go swing.

She found a far corner of the coal store, a long low underground cellar, and made herself an altar. Fire was not permitted in the store, but she didn't care. A hob, uncaring of the flouting of a rule? Unheard of. And yet, here she was. She. Did. Not. Care.

And who would she make a shrine to? Hestia was useless. Had come to her aid but once, and it had cost her dear; that was almost a thousand years ago, now. She thought about what she needed. Retribution. Justice. That would be the goddess Rhamnousia, then. She hoped a hobgoblin incantation to the goddess, a small offering, a shrine, might suffice to garner an audience. Then she'd hope to find something to barter, or trade, to enact her revenge on her kyrios.

"Please, mayst it not be my soul," she thought out loud.

She had built a small table from the ubiquitous wooden packing boxes, upturned, and had stolen some candles from the pottery's gate office in the dark of a night. She lit one candle, waxed onto the upturned crate, and used it to soften and melt another candle. She shaped this with skilled hands, making the winged female form of the goddess Rhamnousia. She took a tiny strip of cloth ripped from her undershirt and bound the eyes of the figurine.

She placed the figurine next to the burning candle, then reached for her precious cup of sour milk, a scant thimble-full remaining, and no more likely to come soon. Her stomach rumbled with longing, even though it was spoilt. She poured the few drops onto the floor, a libation.

Then she closed her eyes, stilled her mind, and reached inside for the memory of the old language, taught to her so long ago that the meaning of the words was lost; just the form, the sound, remained. Taking a shuddering breath, worry, hunger and determination warring in her belly, she spoke the incantation. Opened her eyes. Nothing appeared changed. The candle flickered in a slight breeze on the altar. The figurine of Rhamnousia remained as it had been. Kurra waited, ears and eyes straining for an answer to her call. Nothing. A sob crept up her throat and escaped, hiccupping sideways from her mouth.

She crumpled onto the black, dusty floor, misery and defeat flooding her.

A pressure change, the faintest shift of air, made the hairs on the back of her neck prickle. Someone was behind her. Had John found out where she was hiding? She turned, trying to keep herself as hidden and small as possible. Rhamnousia stood in the crowded space of the cellar. Behind her, iridescent black wings stretched from one side to the other, brushing the dirty walls. She had her hands on her wide hips and her head cocked to one side, showing a smile. An intricately embroidered black veil covered her eyes and the upper half of her face. A faint light emanated from her skin as if she were lit from inside. She wore a great swirl of black baroque cotton with a knot of cloth binding it at her hips.

Kurra abased herself before the goddess, who tutted.

"Kurra of Cazmielou, daughter of Kochonitze, stand before your goddess." The command spoke directly into Kurra's mind. And so she stood, turning her head away in trepidation. "Do not turn your face. Look at me!"

She turned, fear clawing at her mind, and looked upon Rhamnousia, goddess of fortune, justice and retribution. Kurra's legs turned to jelly. She could hardly stand and started shaking, her teeth chattering as if she were standing naked in the frozen north. She tried as best she could to utter her supplication, as she had practised.

"G-great goddess, I thank thee f-for heeding mine call. I-I ..." She ran out of steam. *This is a poorly thought-out, and badly executed plan,* she mused.

The goddess looked at her, a fierce gaze examining every aspect of the hob, though Rhamnousia's eyes remained bound by the black veil.

"I see into your soul, little hobgoblin. I see the hurt and angst you carry. Poor Joseph Foden, a young life snuffed out." She used a sing-song tone as if Joseph's death had been of no import at all. "And your current master, John Francis. A drunkard and a fool," she scoffed. "Finally, of course, you will never forget, nor forgive, the Pope of the New God" – she spat the name – "and his house-staff in Avennio Cavarum. But they are all dead, little hobgoblin. All gone to dust and forgotten. Even Joseph Foden will be forgotten, in time. Even brutal John Francis, who seems to have had a sudden change of fortune, will be consigned to the ever-growing list of disregarded humans."

Kurra was petrified in place, could not look away, could not speak. She trembled and tried to keep control of her bladder.

"I see into your soul. Your mind. You wish retribution on John Francis. For his slights against you, for his brutality, and mistreatment? Do you know the meaning of hubris, little hobgoblin? You may speak." She flicked her fingers towards Kurra.

"Great goddess Rhamnousia, I do know the meaning of 'ubris. It be when thou art overly prideful, or ... or too confident in thysen. And then boastful 'bout it."

"Are you not confident, little hobgoblin? To call me to this ..." She seemed to gaze at the sooty walls of the low dim space, though it was difficult for Kurra to understand how, since the goddess's eyes were obscured. "This ... cellar, as if you have something you can offer me, in return for, what, exactly?"

"I offer my service, an' my thanks, an' my devotion, an' ..." Her voice trailed off, doubt assailing her at every side.

"If all hobgoblins were tired of their station, as you are, would I not have an army of supplicants all about me? Do you see them, little hobgoblin?"

"Beggin' thy pardon, My Lady, but I do not see them. P'raps it be that there are so few hobs left that I be your only choice?" As the words left her lips, Kurra knew she had made a mistake. She clamped her large hairy hand over her mouth, but it was too late. The words swam away, delivering their message to Rhamnousia's ears. Or, maybe she had already read Kurra's mind? The goddess smiled, but it was all teeth, and the teeth were pointed, sharp.

"Do not forget, little hobgoblin, what happens to people who exhibit hubris in the presence of their gods. As for your desire to see ill befall John Francis, you might wonder if anyone else hereabouts worships me? Anyone else hereabouts knows the old words that bring and bind? Anyone else who, whilst being a drunkard, doesn't actually think they are any better than a drunkard?"

Kurra drooped. Of course, Rhamnousia had given John the words to bring her into his service. She remembered now. The tattoo on John's brawny forearm, the winged woman, freshly inked without skill or elegance, but inked, nonetheless.

Rhamnousia laughed, a sound that lacked mirth and had all the heaviness of clay.

"Oh, fret not, little hobgoblin. All this shall pass. You will be rid of him, for he will gain exactly what he asked of me, nothing more, and certainly nothing less. You, however ..." Her face darkened, a frown squinting the skin of her cheeks. "You, it seems, are bound up with the Fates. They have their greedy eyes upon you, for their own means and ends. I would say that great things are expected of you, but you are just a hobgoblin. You are already at the bottom of the ladder, and it seems, can't fall any further."

LATER THAT WEEK, THE kiln was ready to be fired once more. The potters had delivered their wares. The saggers were stacked, taller than a house, one atop the other, side by side in a great circle inside the kiln. John was there, overseeing the stacking, in good humour and for once not yet drunk. Kurra screwed up her courage into a white-hot knot inside her and approached him, sideways, holding her shovel up over her chest as a barrier to the man.

"Beggin' thy pardon, sire, might I ask a question?"

John looked at her, for once hatred not the foremost emotion. Derision, maybe, this time. Kurra swallowed.

"Is that not a question already? Stupid hob."

"Aye, sire, it be." She could delay no more and leapt in. "What is it that sire asked of the goddess Rhamnousia?" She closed her eyes, fearful of his reaction.

"Oh, are you consorting with the gods an' goddesses then, behind me back?" he asked, turning to her. She cowered lower behind her shovel. "Well, I'll tell you what my bargain with Rhamnousia is. I asked her for success in the business, such that I could always afford a drink. She gave me you, the spell to bind you, a worker for free worth the same as five men. Plus, she guaranteed a line of potters wanting my services. She said by the seventh kiln firing I'd be able to drink my own weight in whiskey." He laughed at this thought.

Kurra considered what John had said of the pact. "What, then, does Rhamnousia get from the bargain?" she asked, though she thought she knew. She'd said, "He will gain exactly what he asked of me." She was doing this simply for spite!

"You 'ave too many questions, whore hob! Get shovelin'." He lunged at her, the movement sudden, unexpected. The flat of his hand hit the shovel, smashing it into her face. She cried out, spangled dots swimming in her vision, her nose a mess of pain and blood. Another blow caught her in the chest, knocking the breath from her. She staggered backwards, holding the shovel up to ward off further blows, but John just spat at her, snarling, "Get on with it!" before whirling around and walking away with fury in his stride.

She thought about what Rhamnousia had said. "Seven firings, an' thou shalt have all the whiskey you can drink, John Francis."

Chapter 3

The call enfolded her. Lifted the veil that shrouded her, like a gentle breeze caressing the lightest silk. Insistent, persistent, soft.

'Come back to this world. Listen! We have something for you. You are needed. You are required. We love you. Come! Come back!'

"I don't wanna come back. Bugger off, the lot of thou."

She tried to get back to sleep. Or whatever it was that stood in for sleep, in this between place. Between the worlds. Between the realities. Between the lives. It didn't work. The call continued.

'Wake up! You are needed. There is a job to do. A life to help. They need you. Come! Come!' The voice was sibilant, deliciously persuasive, honeyed.

Kurra opened one eye, slit-wise. Realised as she did so that this very action of waking, looking, listening, had brought her back to the world she had left so long ago.

As she lay in her repose, memories rolled into her mind, unbidden. How long ago had it been, now? It felt like over a hundred years had passed since the Potteries. Since the beatings. Since the failed deal with Rhamnousia. Since the seventh kiln firing, and John's drinking so much whiskey that he passed out, and then died a violent, sudden death.

"Feck and buggerin' nonsense," she snapped, opening both eyes to peer into the gloom. "Where the bleeding 'ell am I now? I 'ates this, all this muckin' around, being pulled from pillar to post. Bleedin' Fates. Bugger off back to thine 'ole and stay there."

She stretched out, pushing against the old cloth rags and sawdust and metal shavings and ... she sniffed. Patted the muck on the floor next to her, then held her hand to her nose and smelled her fingers.

"Flippin' mouse blood and rat guts." She pushed the detritus from her body, brushing, with little effect, at her tatty clothes. Then stood and banged her head on the low ceiling. "This ain't," she said with anger and despair, stooping and rubbing her head, "ain't how I were expectin' to wake. Thou couldst've made the roof a tad higher."

She looked about her then, taking in her surroundings properly. She was at the back of a cupboard that was full of dust and cobwebs, squares of rags and mildewed leather, metal cogs and springs. Peering into the lighter area beyond the open front of the cupboard, she saw a workshop – maybe, she thought, a tool store of some type, dim lit from a ceiling fanlight and littered with strap-bound boxes, machine parts, tubs of fasteners. Hand tools were strewn, uncared for, on overflowing workbenches. Larger machines loomed against a far wall, lumbering and monstrous and implacable, swarf and metal shavings spilling from them onto the floor.

"Well, this place is a right mess, an' no mistake. Bleedin' 'ell, I 'ope there's whiskey in the milk. Hah. Or maybe it could be cream. Well, now, no need to be hopeful. It will be milk, at least. Not water." Shaking her head and shuddering at the thought of it being water, she crawled to the edge of her hideaway hole, cautious as a cat. Peered left and right, up and down. The rest of the room, she noticed, was much the same, and threatened to be more disorganised and untidier in the further, unseen reaches.

There was a chipped, white china saucer of milk on the dirty floor in front of the cupboard. She inched forward, leant over it and sniffed. No whiskey.

She pulled away, her movements strained, reversing all the way to the far recesses of the space, against the rear wall of the cupboard. Rested her back, looked out at the debris of the room, and considered her options. Sighed.

"I can take the milk," she thought out loud, "an' that's me bound to whatever scrote set it down, then they gets to decide what to do to me ... be like the Potteries all over again, that will."

You're enslaved to the milk. Pathetic ... muttered a voice in the back of her mind. Kurra thumped her head, making her eyes swim.

"Get out of my head, whoever thou art," she muttered. She shook her head again, trying to clear her thoughts. The milk *was* calling to her, that was certain. It fizzed in her brain, pulled at her limbs. She slapped herself, hard, across the face.

"Ow. That 'urt. Helped though." She laughed, low and guttural. "Or, I can go back to sleep. Fat chance of that." She scratched under her hair; her scalp itched. "Or I can run, this time, an' be free." She looked around at the flotsam filling the cupboard.

"Least I can tidy up in 'ere while I weighs up me options. Can't 'urt." She leant into her hobgoblin soul and reached for the slow time. Did time slow down? Or did she speed up? Or was it all relative? Other hobs were adamant that they slowed time, but Kurra wasn't sure.

When she leant into the slow time, it was like all the energy in the world was available to her. Precision, with extra senses. She couldn't stay there for many minutes, and that was only a few seconds from an outsider's point of view, but during those seconds ...! Time, literally, flew. She stepped in.

Dust motes paused their arbitrary dance. A grubby brown mouse making a tentative foray along a shelf on the far side of the workshop froze in place.

In what seemed to her a few minutes, and to the mouse an instant, she tidied up the inside of the cupboard. She swept out with an old paintbrush, fashioned a sleeping mat out of rags, and a chair and table from parts and boxes and a short, thin piece of wood.

She sat on her chair and re-engaged with the normal flow of space and time, the dust motes resuming their deosil dance, the mouse, oblivious, whiskering for danger and food.

"What to do, what to do," she repeated over and again, hoping that this simple mantra would yield an answer. The milk continued to make its presence known, a constant reminder, a temptation, a desire, a craving. Kurra shut her eyes, plugged her long, pointed ears with her fingers, tried to block out the siren call. Started to rock backwards and forwards, a terrible pressure building in her chest.

She came back to herself, satisfied, replete. Wiped the creamy milk from her mouth with the back of her hand.

Belched. Realisation struck. She sprawled on the filthy floor by the saucer. The saucer was licked clean.

"Oh, Great Goddess. Why? Why am I enslaved by this curse?!" she railed at the walls and the high vaulted roof of the workshop and beat her fists on the floor, raising clouds of sooty dust. Tears started down her leathery face, and she hauled herself back up into her new home, bereft and saddened and hollow from her loss of freedom. She flung herself onto her makeshift, ragged bed.

You are enslaved, you are. What do you expect, after what you've done? whispered the wheedling voice inside her skull.

She tried to plug her ears, to no avail. Exhaustion overtook her.

"WHAT ARE YOU DOING here, Chidiebere Adebayo?" she asked herself, looking in the cracked mirror in the factory's ladies' loo. The girl in the mirror – afro hair in a tight bun, pebble glasses in cheap blue plastic frames, brown eyes made huge by the spectacles – stared back. She tried a smile. Her teeth were nice, she supposed. But really. "What are you doing here? The only black girl for twenty miles, trying to become a CNC machinist?" She scoffed at herself, at her mam's ideas. At it all, really. She washed her hands, dried them on the ragged towel. Sniffed it. That needed a wash, as well. She'd take it home and launder it.

Mind, there was always her little experiment. A frisson of excitement bubbled in her chest. Silly, really, when she thought about it. Magic. Faeries. Brownies and hobs ... who was she kidding? Spoilt milk from being left out all night on the floor, more like. She scoffed at herself again.

But ... there were tales, about her grandmam. Her mam said the things her mother had got up to, the tales she told, and it made Chi's chest ache with excitement. In the end, who really knew anything? She shrugged, hurried out of the loo and into the corridor.

BUSTLING INTO THE TOOLING storeroom, she stuttered to a halt. The saucer was empty. Not just empty. She peered. Licked clean. To the best of her knowledge, there were no cats in the factory. So ... she leant down, one hand on the worktop above the cupboard, and squinted into the gloom. There was a table, fashioned from an upturned packing box. A chair, a pile of bedding. All sized for a being of about two feet tall. The bedding stirred and rustled.

"Oh my fucking God, it worked!" She yelped, jumping back, excitement coursing through her, making her scalp tingle. A small, thin, raggedy figure rolled out of the tiny bed and shrank away at the back of the cupboard. It looked up at her with large, cautious eyes.

"Aye, it worked. Thou shalt keep a civil tongue, lass. What dost they call thee?" The voice was of a lower pitch than Chi would have thought for the size of person. Being. Thing. Gravelly, with a Midlands brogue.

"Oh! Sorry. I'm Chidiebere. People here call me Chi." She looked left and right, then; they were definitely alone. "I'll get a bollocking if Jamie finds out about you. Oh my God, I can't believe it worked!" She let out a squeak, unable to contain her excitement. Her mam would be ecstatic! Then, remembering her manners; "Oh! What's your name? Are you allowed to tell me? Or should I even ask? And, are you a brownie? A hob? What are you?"

The creature raised an eyebrow. It looked ... female? She was slight of frame, barefoot, her feet and hands disproportionally large and hairy. She was dressed in ragged clothes, patched and dirty. A faded red strip of cloth was tied about her waist. Her long grey hair was pulled back with ancient hair grips, which partially hid pointed ears. Her face, thin and angular, held expressive deep brown eyes, which regarded Chi with patience. Chi stopped fidgeting and talking.

The creature stood, as tall as the cupboard under the workbench would allow. Took a deep breath. Bowed.

"Thou canst call me Kurra, or hob, Chidiebere-ma'am. And I am a hob, aye."

"Oh, please, call me Chi."

"Thy name is Chidiebere. I has to call thee that, or ma'am, Chidiebere-ma'am. It's the rules, see?"

Chidiebere felt heat rising on her face; she felt abashed. Rules? Who knew there were rules?

"I'm so sorry, I really don't know what I'm doing. Me mam has this old book, you see, it was my grandmam's, and it has this spell, and ..." She sighed. "There's so much cleaning up to do. The blokes, they never let me do anything, not good stuff like running the CNC mill or anything, all I get to do is sweep the fucking ... sorry, the flipping floor. And make tea. Endless ... flipping cups of tea."

Kurra leant against the cupboard's back wall, amusement flickering in the curve of her lips.

"Thou 'ast called me, an' I'm bound to thee. I will clean. And mend. And serve. That is my function, after all. Thou wilt show me where, and it shall be done."

Just as Chi went to reply, Jamie's voice echoed down the hallway outside.

"Oi! Chi! Where's that tea?"

Chidiebere jerked back, her eyes panic-wide behind her glasses. He sounded impatient, as usual. She looked back at the hob. "Gotta go! See ya later!" she whispered. Then, "Coming, Jamie!" she shouted over her shoulder. She stood and rushed away, heading for the staff kitchen.

Chapter 4

"I brought you a pot of cream. It's only single. But me mam says you'll like it, better than milk. That right?" She set the pot down next to Kurra, who was sitting on the edge of the workbench above her cupboard, heels idly drumming the cabinet front below. Kurra reached for the pot, picked it up by her fingertips, and turned it this way and that, regarding it as if it were alive, or dangerous.

"This be cream?" She sniffed it, then. "It smells of ... of plass-tick." She pronounced the new word with deliberation, rolling it around in her mouth, testing its feel and sense.

"Yeah." Chi smiled. "Here, you pull the lid back, use that little tab, watch." She put her hands over Kurra's, held the pot and peeled back the lid, taking care to keep the whole on an even keel. Kurra's eyes widened at the sight of the white cream inside. She inhaled, filling her lungs, the heavy sweet scent suffusing her mind with euphoria.

"Goddess, that does smell good." She snaked her tongue out and slurped some of the cream. Her whole body shuddered in appreciation and rapture at the taste. "I thank thee, Chidiebere-ma'am."

"Well, thank *you*, Kurra. Look at this place! It's spotless!" Chidiebere's face was plastered with a wide smile, her eyes sparkling. Kurra looked at the workshop, or storeroom, or whatever it was. It had been a few days, and the dirt was mostly taken care of. The swarf and dust and cobwebs were cleared. The hand tools were back in their boxes or hanging on hooks or nails on the wall, their edges honed, their bearings oiled. She had cleaned the high fanlight, and the room flooded with light, sun dappling the swept floorboards. She was reasonably content. There were still a few items that needed attention. But as a start, it was good. She eyed the doorway to the rest of the factory. Soon she would range further.

"I be glad thou art happy with my work, ma'am."

"Yeah." Chidiebere giggled. "Jamie can't get his head around it. Makes me chuckle. I told him I got a ghost spirit to help me. He just laughed at that. Oh! And, guess what?"

"I cannot guess, ma'am."

"Cos I got ... well, cos you got everything cleaned up, they have no more excuses, and I get to run the milling machine!" Her eyes creased at the corners and her grin became wide. Kurra felt a welling up of pride in her chest.

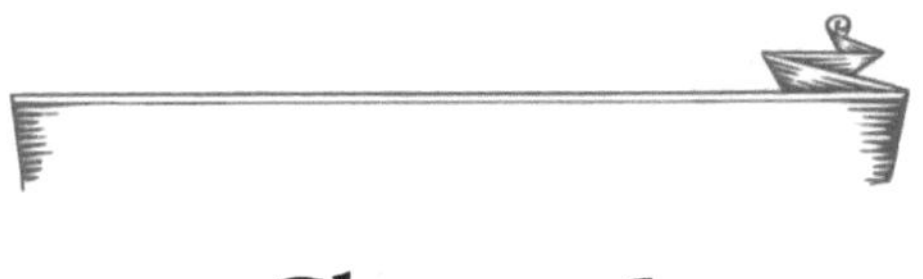

Chapter 5

"Kurra ... you there?" Chi's voice was soft, almost a whisper.

"Chidiebere-ma'am," Kurra replied, moving through her slow time to appear instantly in front of Chidiebere, who was bending down to peer into Kurra's cupboard.

"Shit!" Chi exclaimed, jumping back. "You scared me!"

"I apologise. Thou called me, and so I came. Though it be Sunday; I were not expectin' thee."

Chi looked flustered but pushed her glasses back against the bridge of her nose, using the habit to compose herself, and straightened up. "Sorry, did you need a day off? Or could you, would you come with me out of the factory?"

"If thou commands it, I can, willingly."

"Well, I command it. Please come with me. Me mam's asked me to drop in on her friend to fix her roof, or her plumbing, or possibly both, and I need a helper. You OK with that?"

"Aye, I can fix roofs. Plumbing, not so much."

"Cool. We can learn together. Come on!" She walked away towards the door of the tooling store. Kurra paused for a moment, shrugged and followed.

She looked around the factory with interest as they walked from "her" room, the one Chi had summoned her into, and into the main factory. It was a huge echoing space, metal framed, filled with machinery and hulking dark assemblies that were at various stages of construction. One side of the space was lined with a metal store, great long lengths of steel on racks, plate steel on pallets of wood resting on the scuffed concrete floor. Chi led the hob through the echoing machine floor and to a human-sized side door set into the steel frame of the building. Kurra noticed the enormous sliding doors along the front of the building; large enough for the things being built inside to be loaded onto carts. Chidiebere stepped through into the brightness of the day outside; Kurra paused, uncertainty gnawing at her. She wrung her hands. Chi stuck her head back inside.

"You OK?"

"I ain't sure."

"Is it that you can't leave the building?" Chi's forehead creased with concern.

"Nay, Chidiebere-ma'am, it ain't that. But I han't been outside in this world for a long time."

Chi stepped back into the factory and held out her hand. "Come on. We'll walk together. My car is just there." She pointed through the door. Kurra took her hand; Chi's skin was soft and warm. It made Kurra confident, her kyrios being so close, and, as she had felt from the very beginning, she was a good person. Kind.

Outside, the light was so bright that Kurra used her other hand to shield her eyes. And again, she stuttered to a halt, despite Chi's tug on her arm. They had emerged from the door onto an area where the ground wasn't cobbled, or dirt, as Kurra was used to, but black, and smooth, with white lines on it. Wheeled-metal-and-glass machines stood on the black surface. The heat of the sun was strong, making the black ground smell of pitch, or coal tar. It must be summer, thought Kurra.

"Come on. My car's this one here." Chi pointed at one of the machines, its sides dented and dirty, the blue of the paint rusting in places. She opened the door, and Kurra saw there were seats inside.

"A carriage? Where, then, is the 'orse?"

"Oh, you're not from round here, are you?" asked Chi, laughter in her voice. When Kurra looked nonplussed, Chi laughed aloud. "It's a joke. An old saying that country folk would say of city folk."

"Aye, the sayin' is common enough. And nay, I ain't from 'ere, I reckons."

"Get in." Chidiebere was still holding the door open. Though Kurra was dubious about the conveyance's ability to move without obvious means, she climbed inside and settled on the seat. Chi slammed the door and walked around to the opposite side, climbing into her own seat, which sat behind a large wheel and an array of instrumentation and levers. A look of amusement passed over Chi's face. "You should probably have a booster seat ... hang on." She leant over and rummaged behind them, turning up a coat so bright it offended Kurra's eyes. Chi folded the coat into a pad. "Sit on this. It will lift you up a bit. Seat belt, like this, see?" She showed Kurra where the seat belt was, how it buckled into the metal and ... plas-tick, that stuff again. Kurra was amazed, the material showed up everywhere. It was as if she had been transported to this world from another. She supposed being asleep beyond the world for so long, it was a bit like travelling through time to the future.

When the engine started, Kurra felt a glimmering of terror but tried not to show it. She gripped the edge of her seat with strong, large fingers, however, and Chi must have noticed the white of her knuckles.

"Hey, it's OK, we're only going up to the next village. Try to relax." She gave a smile that Kurra felt was trying to be supportive, but really, this was beyond any of her previous experiences.

Once they were moving, progressing along the smooth strips of black that seemed to have been laid over the dirt tracks and cobbled byways that Kurra would expect, she calmed, by degrees. The sight of trees and grass, fields, hedges, things that were constant for the hobgoblin in her life, calmed her more. Though they whipped past at such a velocity she felt they would surely be flattened. After what seemed a long time to the terrified hob, but she realised later was probably merely minutes, they turned off the main thoroughfare with its other horseless conveyances. They were swallowed up by the hedges bordering a tiny track that was muddy and rutted, which was more the sort of environment Kurra was comfortable within. Plus, the conveyance had slowed to a much more reasonable velocity.

"You OK, Kurra?"

"Aye, ma'am. It be good to see the green of the trees."

"We'll be there in a minute. Um. I'm guessing you're difficult for people to see? I mean, Jamie's never seen you, right?"

Kurra thought of the large, loud factory owner. She wasn't sure if Master Britten saw much that was beyond the end of his self-centred nose.

"Master Britten dun't 'ave the sight, nay, ma'am. He sees nought but what he wants to see."

"Yeah, thought so. Well. Josephine's a ... I'm not sure what she is. Different. I think she's got the sight, as you call it. So. Well. Oh! We're here." She pulled on the wheel, that which directed the conveyance, and they turned off the narrow track into a cleared area in front of a low red-brick cottage. The garden before it was fecund with plants, all higgledy-piggledy, growing with furious abandon and no sense of order. It made Kurra's teeth itch. The cottage itself, approached along a paved pathway through the garden that was overgrown on both sides, looked careworn and patched, the grimy windows open to the summer heat. There was a hole in the roof, which looked, to Kurra's eye, as if it had been blown out from inside. Jagged chunks of tile littered the path that ran along the front of the building. Some of them had witness marks that looked charred, the edges glassy, as if from extreme heat. Kurra raised an eyebrow but said nothing.

A woman in a full, deep-russet dress, her white hair cascading down her back, strode around the corner of the house. She was carrying a long, dark wooden staff, topped with a curious brass three-pointed object, inscribed with a spiral. Kurra felt power resonating within the staff, and she halted, shrinking against the wall of the cottage.

"Hi, Josephine!" called Chi, waving. "We ... uh, I've come to look at your roof. Me mam sent me. Uh, Obi Adebayo ... I'm Chidiebere. Um, people call me Chi ... um ..." Chi ran out of steam. Josephine had stopped in her tracks and was staring at Kurra, who was doing her best to hide behind Chidiebere's legs. Kurra looked at Josephine, who returned her gaze with deep, dark, wise eyes set in a weathered brown face, laughter creasing her eyes' corners.

"Oh, kushti divvus, mistress hob, please be welcome and safe on my land," she said, her voice deep and soft, melodic. She had the sight, thought Kurra. Kurra bowed her thanks but didn't dare speak.

"Um, you can see Kurra, then?" asked Chi, worry washing over her face.

Josephine looked at Chi, then. "Aye, I can see her. You're Obi's girl, come to fix the roof, then?" Her smile broadened. "Reckon we need a cup of tea, first, though. It's almost elevenses after all. Follow me." And she swirled her dress around, marching off back to the corner of the cottage.

"Well, that's a turn-up for the books, eh, Kurra?" Chidiebere laughed.

"Aye, ma'am. Tis that." Though Kurra didn't relax. Too much was different and new. Uncertainty tugged at her thoughts.

They followed Josephine along another overgrown path down the side of the cottage. The back garden was mostly an ancient orchard, deep with grasses and shrubs, a kitchen garden set at one side in which runner beans, raspberries and courgettes were doing their best to escape into the main garden – huge leaves, suckers, tendrils all making a break for it. Josephine ignored the cottage and walked through the orchard, along a well-worn path made from the same red bricks, ducking under an ancient apple tree's branches. Kurra and Chi followed, and they emerged into a tiny clearing.

The grass here was shorter, an attempt had been made at mowing, or maybe, thought Kurra, there were sheep involved. In the centre of the clearing stood a horse-drawn caravan, its shafts resting on a pair of bricks, its green tarpaulin stretched tight over the curved roof, weathered and stained in places. The paintwork was faded and old; the brushwork on the door depicting a pair of great horses was worn and dirty.

A set of steps led into the caravan, the cream paint on each tread thinning from years of use. Outside on the cleared ground was a small fire circle, delineated with flat stones, embers smouldering in the centre. Over the fire hung a large soot-blackened kettle, the chain supporting it attached to a pole that had been thrust into the ground. Josephine set about adding kindling and small twigs to the fire to bring the kettle to the boil.

"Oh wow! This is cool!" exclaimed Chi, taking in the caravan, the fireplace and the clearing. They were surrounded on all sides by dense fruit trees, their summer foliage providing a welcoming shade from the heat of the sun.

"Sit yersens down, lasses," Josephine commanded, busying herself at the fire and with mugs for tea.

Kurra stood. She wrung her hands and jogged from one foot to the other as Chi settled onto a spindle-backed chair, one of four that sat arranged by the fire. Josephine noticed Kurra's distress, and turned square to her, bowing.

"Kurra, be seated at my hearth. You are welcome and safe. You may eat and drink here, without obligation."

The tension that had stiffened Kurra's posture dissolved, eased away by the warmth behind Josephine's words. She recognised Josephine as chivani, a Romani witch. There had been a similar travelling wise-woman … when? The court of the Karamanian, Ibrahim Bey. Six hundred years ago. She bowed to Josephine in return, her movements stiff and formal.

"I thank thee for thine assurances, ma'am. Be there owt I can assist with?"

Josephine smiled. "No, just be seated, we will drink tea. Or would you prefer milk?"

Kurra's heart leapt. She liked this chivani more and more as the minutes passed.

"Oh, milk will go down a treat." Chidiebere laughed. "Just don't give her cream if you want her to help with the roof; it makes her go all googly-eyed."

Kurra felt a slight reddening of her skin.

"Googly-eyed, Chidiebere-ma'am?"

"You go all weird. Think it affects your brain."

"It's so delicious!" Kurra started to vibrate at the thought of another pot of cream.

"Well." The witch grinned. "I do see what you mean, Chidiebere, about it making her go funny. Anyroad, I haven't got no cream, but there's milk. I'll fetch it in a minute."

The fire, now a hot blaze, was starting to boil the kettle, and smoke was rising through the branches of the apple trees. Josephine set the mugs out, climbed the steps into the caravan and returned with a glass pint bottle of milk, its sides dewed with condensation. Kurra eyed it and licked her lips, anticipation swelling in her chest.

"So," started Chi. "Mam said you need your roof fixing, and maybe the plumbing?" She raised her eyebrows in query, looking over at the cottage, just visible through the overgrown garden.

"There was a leak, in the pipes in the loft. I wove a draba – eh, a spell, a simple thing – to bind the pipes. It ... well, it didn't so much bind the pipes as ... well, escape. Escape through the roof. I think it was afraid."

"Your spell escaped?" Chi's eyebrows shot up in part disbelief, part amusement.

Josephine looked down at the fire. "I don't usually try to enchant things, you know, pipes, plumbing, inanimate stuff. Beings are so much easier. Well, to start with, at least. I'm still barred from the White Swan." She looked up, grinning at them. "Never mind about that! Now then. Tea. Sugar, Chidiebere?" She reached for the kettle and poured water into two mugs, adding a generous glug of milk into the third.

Kurra couldn't take her eyes off the mug of milk and almost leapt at it as Josephine handed it to her. She guzzled it down, making slurping noises in her delight.

"She really does go googly-eyed, doesn't she?" remarked Josephine, her voice rustling with dry humour.

Kurra looked at them both over the rim of her mug, holding it so she could at least hide part of her face. She used her tongue to lick milk from her top lip.

"I thank thee, once again, Josephine, ma'am," she mumbled, embarrassed.

KURRA LEANT INTO HER slow time and pulled on the extra ability it gave her to balance, then stepped off the ladder and out onto the slope of the roof of the cottage, her broad bare feet gripping the edges of the tiles. She looked up at a house sparrow, almost within her reach above her head. The movement of its wings was perceptible to her, a slow sweep of the air as the bird itself hung almost motionless. Shrugging, she looked at the job at hand. It was straightforward enough in her hobgoblin mind, the structures and methods of roofing not having substantively changed in a thousand years. She stripped back the old tiles, carrying them down the ladder a pair at a time, piling them on the path at the front of the cottage. She replaced the broken rafters and purlins, the laths and battens, using timber that the chivani had collected in a corner of her orchard. She cut it to length with a hand saw, nailed it in place, all the while using her slow time to increase her agility and carpentry ability. She worked around the stationary form of Chi, who had pulled out a great bag of plumbing tools from her conveyance and was inside the loft space working on repairing a copper pipe.

Before she started replacing the tiles, she stepped back into real time. Chi looked up, astonishment writ large across her face.

"You fixed the rafters already?!" she exclaimed. "You're amazing."

"I am hob, ma'am. Just a hob."

"Even so. I think it's amazing. I mean, you're almost done; I'm only just starting."

"I can help if thou needst?"

"I thought you didn't know plumbing?"

"I 'ast a keen mind, ma'am. I can see the shape of it. Though if I replace the tiles first, dost thou 'ave the … elecktrik light?" She stumbled over the new word. So many new words!

Chi smiled. "Yes, I have a light, Kurra. Please, let's get the tiles fixed so the roof is waterproof."

Kurra leant back on her slow time and fetched more unbroken tiles from the "spares stack", as Mistress Josephine had called it, two at a time. And the tiles she had taken and stacked by the path. Each one she positioned, nailing it onto its batten, and in short order, the roof was sealed against the elements.

She took a moment to sit on the roof of the cottage, in her bubble of space-time, looking out over the silent landscape, the frozen insects, the unmoving animals, the birds in flight, interrupted. It was a pleasant environment. So much better than the Potteries, or that goddess-forsaken cotton mill.

"Hah," she scoffed to herself. "Goddesses. Last time I'm muckin' about with them." But as she said it, she remembered what Rhamnousia had said. "You, it seems, are bound up with the Fates." Well. She could go swing. Her and the Fates.

She stepped back to real time once more, slid down the ladder and walked through the jumbled rooms of the cottage, up to the loft ladder where she could see the elecktrik illuminating the roof space.

CHIDIEBERE GRUMBLED to herself. She'd done a unit on plumbing at technical college and had all the tools, but she was acutely aware she lacked real-world experience. Not through want of trying. Her mam sent her enough weekend work to keep her busy, and the money was good when it was paid, but really. It was cramped, difficult, often smelly work. Often damp work, if she was honest with herself.

Whatever spell Josephine had employed, it had certainly bound the pipes. It looked like they had been squeezed in the hand of a giant. They were mangled beyond saving. She used a pipe cutter and excised the mess, replacing it with new copper. It was difficult to get the cutter into the space and she skinned her knuckles, muttering and cursing under her breath.

"With what might I assist thee, ma'am?"

Chi looked up, glad of the distraction. Kurra had taken about two seconds to re-tile the hole in the roof. She'd only just turned the battery work lamp on and started cutting, and here Kurra was.

"You're amazing, you know that, right? You fixed her roof, y'know" – she clicked her fingers – "just like that!"

"I can do roofs, I did say."

"I know, I know. Right, I reckon this is assembled now." She indicated the pipework, new sections showing bright copper. "Just need to solder it up." She hefted her blowtorch. Kurra eyed it with caution, took a step back. Chi pressed the button and the torch lit with a bright roaring blue flame.

Kurra shrank back. Chi realised that this might be a step too far for the hob and released the button. The torch extinguished with a pop.

"It's OK, this is a blowtorch. For soldering pipe. Look, you press this button ..." She pressed, and the flame punched out again. And with similar rapidity, it went out. "When you release the button, it goes out. Here, try it." She passed the blowtorch to Kurra, who took it, holding it at arm's length as if it would bite her.

"Right, listen. Flux goes on to make the solder flow. Solder goes on when the brass changes colour. Point the blowtorch at that join and press the button, hold the flame on. Ready?"

"I ain't ready, nay," quailed Kurra, her hand shaking where she held the torch.

"Here, let me," said Chi, putting her hand over Kurra's, as she had with the pot of cream. "Like this ..." And she pressed the button, her finger over Kurra's finger. She moved Kurra's hand so the blowtorch heated the pipe. "See how it changes colour?"

"Yes, Chidiebere-ma'am," Kurra replied, though she was shivering against Chi's front, where they touched. The solder melted into the join and flowed, quicksilver bright against the darkened brass. Chi relaxed her finger over Kurra's finger. The blowtorch stopped. Quiet descended. The loft smelled of heat and the flux filled the air with a tart, rank smell. Kurra leant forward, peering at the soldered join in the pipe, wrinkling her nose. "It smells foul ... though tis akin to magic, My Lady," she whispered, reverence in her voice.

"Yep, and the rate plumbers charge, they may as well be sorcerers!" Chi laughed.

Chapter 6

Kurra didn't like to admit it to herself, but she was starting to enjoy her life. Chidiebere was a good kyrios. The Sunday trips out into the surrounding countryside – sometimes plumbing jobs, often with a visit to the chivani, Josephine, with tea for Chi and milk for her – were a highlight. The factory was now spotless, and she had started on the offices where the designers and accountants worked. The work was easy, the company of Chi and Josephine pleasant, the weather clement as summer rolled into autumn.

This weekday evening, the factory was closed up, silent; Chidiebere had gone home at six, and Kurra had done her rounds. She had cleaned the main part of the building, the tooling store where she had her cupboard, the paint and chemical store, and a couple of other rooms used for more intricate machine assembly and manufacture. Now she was heading to the administrative offices: three long low rooms full of paper, and mechanical thinking machines, full bins and empty coffee cups. As she opened the door to the corridor next to these rooms, the light was spilling through the door at the far end. Master Britten's office. Voices! She shrank back. But she needed to get the bins emptied, the cups cleaned. She had promised Chidiebere. It was, after all, her reason for being.

So she crept in, keeping under the desks, pressing into slow time to cross the corridors or when she didn't have cover. No one would see her. She collected up the wastepaper into a black plas-tick bin bag, put it in the recycling at the back of the building. Went back into the offices for the cups, all stacked neatly onto a tray she carried in one hand, the magic of slow time allowing her extra muscular precision. She deposited the cups in the kitchenette sink, cleaned them and stacked them, wiped the surfaces. All tidy.

Edging back along the corridor, she peered through the crack in Master Britten's door, to see if there were cups to collect, bins to empty. She had done this before, whisked around his office whilst he was sitting, frozen in time, his eyes glued to the screen of his thinking machine. He had noticed something, had mentioned it to Chi in passing the following day ... "It felt like your ghost-thing was in my office last night," he had joked to her, so she said.

But tonight, as evidenced earlier by the voices, there were more people in there than Master Britten. This was unusual, it being the evening. She peered, cautious. Two other people were present. They looked ... different. Different from all the people she had met in this age. But not different from the people of a previous age. Not different from the people at court with the Pope. These were men of the New God! A shudder racked her shoulders. What did they want at a ... she recalled Chi's explanation of what they did here at the factory. What did the men of the New God need from a Manufacturing Pump Engineer?

She slid through the door without displacing it and crouched next to a desk, then re-entered the present time.

"Let me get this straight," Master Britten was saying. "You would like me to build this pump, to be delivered to a place which you can't tell me about, to be installed by us, but to pump a mystery substance you won't tell me about, and you'll pay me in ..." Kurra saw him glance down at his desk, to read notes he must have there. "You'll pay me in 'gold and jewels to the value of three times the market price of the pump'?"

"Yes, that is correct, Mr Britten," replied the man of the New God, who was wearing vestments all in red. A Cardinal, Kurra recalled. His accent sounded Calabrian.

"You'll forgive me for being suspicious? Sounds illegal, what with the mystery location, substance and non-traceable payments?"

"I understand. I can assure you there is no illegality at play here. However, these are our terms, and we insist upon them."

Kurra watched whilst Master Britten contemplated the deal. She looked at the two men of the New God. The Cardinal was a fat, wobble-jowled man of greying, receding hair who smelt of avarice. The thin, stooped, black-enrobed man next to him had the look of a cleric or scribe or ... or an engineer. That propensity to shrink away from others, the interest in the technical drawing on the table before them. He had the stink of machine oil and pencil shavings about him.

As she watched, she became aware of movement behind her. The door! She mashed down on her slow time, all motion around her freezing in an instant. She turned and saw that a third man of the New God was entering the room. He was looking straight at her! Though she had frozen his time, it was clear he had, however briefly, seen her. She noticed in passing that he seemed younger, slimmer, fitter than the other two.

And she could smell ... something on him. Something that smelt of oil and fire and death. He looked dangerous. A soldier? A warrior, certainly. Though a well-dressed one.

She scanned around the room. She wanted to continue to eavesdrop, intrigued and slightly alarmed at the presence of these men of the New God in her factory. Talking to her Master Britten. She climbed onto the desk she was standing next to and leapt for the ceiling, pushing with her fingers so that one of the lightweight tiles of the suspended ceiling flipped up. Above the ceiling tiles, there was a crawl space. It was cramped, airless and dusty. But she would be hidden, and still be able to hear what was discussed. She hoped that the third man would discount her half-seen ghostly form as a figment of his imagination. She hoped. She replaced the ceiling tile behind her and crawled along, using the wire supports and tile frames as hand- and footholds. Until she was directly above Master Britten's desk. The tiles were made from some sort of lightweight fibres pressed into a board; she dug the corner out of one with her fingernail and put her eye to the tiny hole she had created.

As she did this, she ruminated on her actions. Like at the Potteries kiln, what she was doing was against the lore of the hobgoblins – spying on the owner, the employer, the kyrios. Or, at least, the boss of the kyrios. She shrugged. That the New God was involved here bothered her more than the breaking of her own code of conduct. The voice at the back of her head chuckled, ready to add its sarcastic comment. She willed it to be quiet. Now was not the time.

She allowed time to speed back up. Master Britten was still considering what to say in return to the Cardinal. She heard movement from the door as it swung fully open, then shut.

"Credo di aver appena visto un folletto," she heard a gruff voice assert. The young warrior by the door. She screwed up her face in concentration, remembering Calabrian from three hundred years ago. Taking a guess, he'd said, "I just saw a hob." Fear clawed at her as her heart hammered in her chest. She didn't dare even breathe! She remained still, one eye pressed to the hole, hands and feet gripping the tiles' support frame. She could see the desk and the top of Master Britten's head, as well as the black-clad engineer.

"What did he say?" That was Master Britten.

"Eh, do you, er, have a … a spirit, in this place? Maybe something that helps with the cleaning?" The Cardinal. She could almost see his fat jowls wobbling. Oh no! How could they know about hobgoblins? The Pope's service was seven hundred years ago!

Master Britten scoffed. "Our intern thinks there is some sort of ghost or spirit about the place. But really. Ridiculous notion."

"Forgive me. Of course. But I have an interest in the spiritual, as I'm sure you can understand. What is the name of your intern?"

"I'm not sure that is pertinent to the discussion we are having about the pump?"

"I will order five pumps. And pay you ten times the market rate for each one. But I do wish to discuss … spiritual matters … with your intern. As part of the deal. I have only his spiritual well-being at heart."

"*Her* spiritual well-being. Well. This is most irregular. I will need to think on it. Overnight, at the very least."

"That is understandable." The Cardinal's voice was all sugar and smarm. It made Kurra squirm, internally. Externally she was rigid with fear that she would dislodge something, even a mote of dust descending would give her away. She should have cleaned, up here. "Do not delay, however. You are not the only pump manufacturer in the Borders. I will return tomorrow. Please do arrange for me to meet your, er, intern."

Kurra saw the Cardinal's balding pate come into view as he shook Master Britten's hand across the desk. Then the Cardinal and the engineer turned and left her field of view. She heard the door open, and footsteps receding down the hallway, and the door shut. She pushed into slow time and, exhibiting more care than usual, extricated herself from above Master Britten's desk. She scooted along in the cramped space, slid over the wall divider, and dropped down from the ceiling void into the office next door.

She stayed in slow time all the way back to her storeroom and her cupboard, only re-emerging into the normal flow of space and time once she was on her pallet, in her bed, under her covers. She shivered, despite the late-summer warmth of the evening.

Chapter 7

Kurra hung from the chain supporting a light fitting, high above the factory floor. One foot hooked, toes clasping around a chain link, and her strong hands holding the chain against her breast. The light, shining down, would mask her from anyone below who had the sight. She hoped. As she waited, she looked over her domain. She could see the tops of all the machinery. Her heart swelled with pride – even these were free of dust, despite some being so tall that only from this vantage point would a person realise they were completely clean.

She heard a conveyance ... a car, they were called ... arrive on the far side of the doors. She waited. It was still early, but Chidiebere was usually one of the first of the staff to arrive. She hoped today would prove the same.

The side door opened. Kurra's heart sank; it was the dangerous man from the previous evening. He stepped into the factory, closing the door behind him without a sound. He looked left and right, then glanced up towards Kurra's hiding place, squinting against the glare of the lights. Looked away immediately. Then he reached out his hand toward the light switch on the wall next to him. Before he touched it, and whilst he was still looking at his hand, or the switch, Kurra pressed into slow time.

"Hah!" she muttered. "He thinks he's so clever. Well." With the man frozen, almost touching the switch, she climbed up the chain and grabbed the beam below the metal roof. She swung herself across the gap to the wall, using every ounce of her slow time coordination to perform the gymnastic feat without disturbing the chain, or any dust.

Holding the beam at the top of the wall, she paused, looking over her shoulder and down at the doorway. The man was still frozen, still reaching for the switch. Still facing away from her. She slid down the vertical support column and landed with a softness akin to a butterfly's wing. Or so she hoped. She crept amongst the machines and around the factory floor, always keeping something large and opaque between herself and the man. When finally she reached the wide access-way that led between parts of the factory, she ran. She ran past the paint store, past the machine shop, almost past her storeroom and her cupboard.

Realisation flashed in her mind; they would search, they would find her nest, her homely space, in the cupboard. She had time. She ran into the room and pulled her pallet bed out, cast the cloth and rags and padding about randomly. Turned her table the right way up again, so it became a box, then scattered some old tools into the bottom of it. Pushed her stub of a candle back into her space between spaces.

"Well, tis tidier than when I arrived, that much be certain," she observed. Satisfied she had changed her home back into a nondescript, albeit very clean, cupboard, she ran again, for the administration offices and the toilets. The ceiling void was as good a hiding place as any other and had the advantage that she could move between rooms, from the toilets to the offices and back, and eavesdrop on the conversations.

"Though," she mused, as she pulled herself through to the crawl space, "I still ain't cleaned in there, so best be careful. Maybe I have time to do that an' all?"

HAVING CLEANED THE dust from the ceiling void above Master Britten's office, Kurra arranged herself as comfortably as she could, lying on a support beam above the delicate tiles.

Voices! Master Britten, and the Cardinal, and a woman. The door to the offices opened.

"... Really, most irregular," Master Britten was saying with a sigh. "But come in, anyway. I'll put the kettle on; no one else is in yet."

"And when should we expect the, er, intern?" That was the Cardinal. Still angling for Chidiebere! Kurra's heart rate increased.

"She's usually here by now. Have a seat. Tea? Coffee?"

"No, thank you."

"How about you, miss ...?" The inflection of Master Britten's voice indicated a question.

"I do not require a beverage," a thin, sibilant voice announced. It made Kurra's skin crawl. Was that an elven voice? She was sure it was. All she could see was Master Britten's desk.

Kurra felt the familiar fizz in her blood. Chi was close! Her hob ears twitched. Someone had entered the toilet room. She leant into slow time and crept, as careful as a fox, through the ceilings and over to the women's toilets. She relaxed back into real time.

"Chidiebere-ma'am?" she whispered.

"Kurra?" Chi's voice echoed, hollow in the enclosed space.

Kurra prised up a tile and dropped down onto the hand basin, grabbing the edge of the hand dryer to steady herself. Chi's eyes widened; she had been washing her hands but stopped, soapy water dripping from them into the sink.

"Chidiebere-ma'am?" Kurra whispered again. "There are men here from the Church. A Cardinal. And I think an elf, as well. And a soldier, a dangerous man. I ... I don't know what's going on, but I'm right scared. I've been 'iding half the night. The soldier could see me. Think he has the sight."

"Wait, what? What are you on about?" Chi's face was half amused, trying to find the joke, half alarmed, trying to parse what Kurra was saying. "A Cardinal, an elf and a soldier? Sounds like a bad joke."

"Tain't no joke, ma'am. I've met these sort before. Bad Church people. Like the Pope."

"You've met the Pope?"

"No. Yes, um. No. Not this one. One of the old ones. He weren't a nice man."

Kurra's ears picked up the faintest noise outside the washroom door, and she vaulted upwards, pressing into slow time as she did so. She had the tile replaced and her breathing under control in a matter of half a minute, and relaxed into real time again, listening. The washroom door opened.

"Are you Chidiebere Adebayo?" The elven sibilance. Kurra's heart sank.

"Yes. Er, who are you?"

"I am Aedredd, daughter of Aelfgifu, of Neustria. Please, follow me."

Definitely an elf, Kurra thought. Not one she had heard of. Aelfgifu sounded oddly familiar, though. She shrugged. She could hear Chi and the elf leaving the washroom. Footsteps heading towards Master Britten's office.

Chapter 8

"Back an' forth, back an' forth. I shall get dizzy at this rate." Kurra silently remonstrated with herself as she slipped, silent as a cat's paw, through the ceiling space once again. Settled into her watching place once again.

All the people were assembled, scant inches below her hiding place. The terror was trying to make her shiver, and she did her best to stop any outward sign, lest she shake the ceiling tiles or her teeth chatter.

"Ah! Chi. Thanks for popping in," the booming voice of Master Britten started.

"Tell us about the ... helper, the hobgoblin, the, eh, brownie," the Cardinal asked, without preamble. Kurra could almost hear Master Britten's face going puce. But what a question! They were looking for her. Why?

"I say, now then, no one's suggesting—" started Master Britten, but the elf cut him off.

"Be silent. We ask questions. Speak when you are spoken to."

Kurra couldn't see the room, but she could imagine Master Britten opening and closing his mouth in astonishment, could almost see Chi's round eyes widening behind her thick spectacles.

"Chidiebere," Aedredd began. "Tell us where the hobgoblin is now."

Kurra's blood ran cold, and she shivered, unable to control her reaction.

"She's in the ceiling, above the toilets," said Chi. No! Kurra couldn't understand, wouldn't comprehend. Chi had betrayed their secret! Betrayed their bond, had taken no notice of her warning! She mashed into slow time and dashed, uncaring of leaving a trace, for the end of the ceiling space and the hallway. Some force, some elven magic, pulled at her, even in slow time, but she shrugged it off and kept going.

She dropped into the hallway, skidding on the smooth floor and bolted for the fire exit at the far end of the corridor. Nowhere in the factory was safe if they were looking for her. Only her ability to stop time allowed her some advantage. Her heart fluttered in her chest, sweat prickling her scalp as she cast about for a remedy to the situation. Some slim but attainable resolution for her, and for Chidiebere. She pushed down on the crash bar to open the fire door, and light flooded in from the morning sun. Squinting, she slipped through, closing the door with one hand on the jamb to dampen its movement. The door clicked shut. She stepped back into real time.

The roar of traffic, of cars and larger wagons on the roadway, assailed Kurra's ears. But she was at the very rear of the building, where there was a ditch between factory units, a desultory stream, and an understorey of plants. Ferns, anemones, phlox and other shade-loving growth. Spindly ash and prickly hawthorn bushes fought for light. There was a paved access path for humans, but Kurra slipped into the understorey around the stream, allowing its green caress to envelop her.

As she lay, panting, trying to fight the rising panic, the snide voice made itself known again. *Oh yes. Running away from your kyrios. Very brave. You've left her in there, at the mercy of…*

"Shu' up! Leave me alone!" Kurra whispered, clamping her hands over her long ears. The voice receded, laughing, echoing. She shook her head to clear her mind. Now was not the time to be distracted. Chidiebere-ma'am would be OK, she was sure. Was she sure? Worry gnawed at her guts.

She wriggled along, parallel to the watercourse, working her way from the fire exit to the side of the building, and access to the place where Chidiebere would park her car.

She lay in the embrace of the greenery and foliage between the stream and the area where the cars were left during the day. Her mind raced. She dared not use slow time again, sure that the elf had a way to detect it. So she stayed utterly still and watched.

She had a view of the car parking area and the side of the building, with its door, and, away behind her, the fire exit.

The fire exit door crashed open. A tall, androgynous, slim elven figure appeared, wearing a cream linen suit. She looked out at the foliage, the cars, the open sky. As she scanned left and right, her long yellow-blonde hair whipped this way and that. Kurra stayed as silent as she was able, stilling even her breath. She kept her thoughts away from hob magic, she was just a normal being, not magical, not interesting.

A tide of magic, glamour, compulsion, broke over her and she almost moved. Only through pulling inner strength from somewhere she hadn't known she possessed was she able to stop herself from standing and announcing herself.

The elf retreated inside, slamming the door after her. Kurra let out a half gasp, half sob. She'd never been so scared in her life. Well, maybe a couple of times. But it had been a long life. She had to make a plan. Had to move, despite shivers of fear freezing her in her hiding place. She had to get away. But how?

Chapter 9

Chidiebere watched the boiling water cascade from the kettle's scaly spout, watched as it splashed into the mug and mixed with the coffee granules, turning almost black as it swirled and filled. She spooned in sugar from the kilo bag on the counter, casual with her aim. Splashed in some milk from the plastic container, half full. Put the milk back in the small countertop fridge. Realised that Kurra hadn't had milk that morning and took the container out again. Noticed the mess of sugar and instant coffee granules on the worktop and reached for a cloth. Stopped, again. She gripped the edge of the counter and leant onto it, screwing her eyes shut so tight that she saw red stars.

What was going on? She didn't feel right. There was a gap. In her consciousness? Her recent memory. She had been in Jamie's office, hadn't she? And there had been other people there, but ... but she couldn't remember them. Their faces. Their voices. She shook her head. She wasn't drunk, was she? No, it was a Thursday. She hadn't been out last night, she'd been in, studying. She scoffed. She was always in, studying! Drink spiked? The factory wasn't a nightclub, and ... she remembered, she had come in, gone to the loo, chatted with Kurra, then ... something in Jamie's office, and now, here she was. She hadn't had a drink, not even water. So. Not spiked. But she felt … weird.

She shook her head again. Whatever it was, it seemed to be receding. She'd take her drink and the milk and see Kurra. That always brought a cheer to her, the hob was so wise and pithy. She straightened up and set off, mug of coffee and milk container in one hand.

She walked into the tooling storeroom. Something was wrong. Even though Kurra was silent, and could appear and disappear in a blink, the room felt empty. Kurra's presence was gone. She set the mug of coffee and the milk down on the spotless work surface and looked into the cupboard. Kurra's cupboard.

"No!" she exclaimed, half sobbing. "No, you can't just go!" Frantic, she got down on all fours and stuck her head right in the cupboard. The bed was gone. The chair was gone. The table was … just a box, full of knackered hand tools. "You can't go, Kurra … I-I need you …" She hadn't realised until that moment, but she did. An emptiness opened in her heart, and she slipped to the floor, sobbing, clinging to the cupboard front with her hands.

Kurra continued to not be there, and after a minute, Chi stopped feeling sorry for herself and started to think. She heard her mam's voice, deep with her Igbo accent: "Tears are there to water the roots of strength."

"Thanks, Mam. You're right." She took a steadying breath, stood up and began to think. "Pff. Well, if Kurra's gone? She can't be gone, cos I brought her so I keep her until I die. That's the rules, she said. And I'm not dead. So Kurra must be … someplace else. Hope she's OK. I still feel a bit weird." She took a slurp of the coffee, hot and steaming, and set the mug down again. "And Jamie owes me some time off, all that weekend work last month. So. Um. Josephine!"

It was as if a literal lightbulb lit inside her head. She grinned. Josephine would know what to do. Or at least, would have wise words, and tea. She left the rest of her coffee on the worktop with the carton of milk, and spun out of the room, crashing through the fire exit that she had been told countless times not to use. Well, this was an emergency, wasn't it?

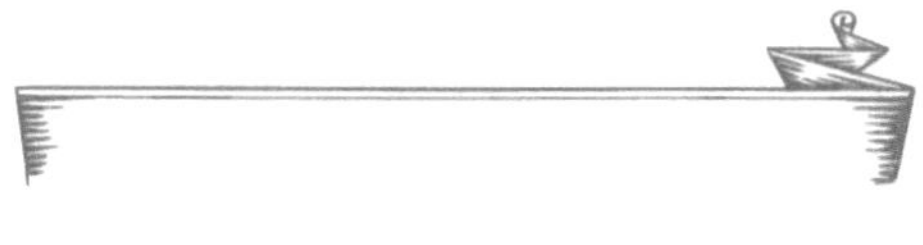

Chapter 10

Chidiebere swung her car into the space in front of Josephine's cottage. Her head was clearing, and she was getting more and more panicked about what had occurred that morning. She was sure that she had been drugged, or coerced in some way, to reveal all that she had said about Kurra. She was also starting to remember parts of what Kurra had said to her. She had spoken of dangerous people and said the old Pope was evil. It didn't make any sense. And what had it to do with her?

She walked around the cottage, feeling the long tendrils of weeds and plants tugging at her calves from the path edges. Josephine's garden was so overgrown! Approaching the orchard, and the vardo, she heard voices. She slowed, uncertainty riding in her heart, then stopped, just beyond the apple tree at the edge of the clearing.

"Someone's here," said a voice, gravelly, the vowels swelling with an eastern brogue.

"It's Chidiebere Adebayo. She's the girl I was telling you about. Her with the hob." That was Josephine's voice. "Come in, Chi, kettle's on!" she called, raising her voice, though Chi was close enough to hear.

Chi ducked under the branch and walked into the clearing. Josephine was, as usual, fussing around the fire and the kettle.

Three mugs were set out. An elderly lady in a voluminous, much-patched emerald-green cloak was sitting on one of the chairs. Her carved walking staff lay over her lap, and her white hair escaped her cloak's hood and furled down her back. She regarded Chi with twinkling blue-grey eyes.

"You're Obi's gal, then? I recognise the similarity, like." She chortled. But stopped laughing when she saw Chi's expression darken. "Now then, don't be gettin' your kecks in a twizzle. What I means is that you looks like your mam. Your facial features, not the colour of your skin."

Chi was taken aback by the brash and forthright turn the conversation had taken but was relieved that this woman didn't seem overtly racist. She had a broad accent ... Fenland? Out that way. Was she a witch, as well? And she knew her mam?

"Yes, I'm Chidiebere, Obi Adebayo's daughter. Pleased to meet you ... um ...?"

"Sorry!" called Josephine, rummaging in the doorway of the vardo. "This is Bobe Elka, she's ... eh. What are you, Elka?" Bobe Elka shrugged, showing her hands to the sky. "She's sort of the patron saint of travellin' folks, or something. We all know her, an' she's pretty wise, and ... well. Ah! Here it is." Josephine straightened up, holding a bottle of milk, speckled with dew as usual. On previous visits, Chi had glanced into the vardo and could never detect any sort of refrigerator or power supply. So where the cold bottles of milk were coming from was, to her, a mystery. When she saw the milk her heart sank, as she remembered the reason she was there.

"You'd best sit yersen down afore you fall down," commented Bobe Elka, waving at a chair. "You look like you needs to pukker your chattle."

Chi was confused but sat on the chair, letting out a sigh, and tried not to cry.

"She means, tell us your woes," Josephine translated.

"Oh. Oh, well ... um ..." As Chi was stuttering, Josephine set the bottle of milk on the low table by the fire. It was too much. Chi burst into tears.

"Kurra's gone, and it's all my fault, and I don't know what I did, and I don't know where she is!" she wailed, eyes screwed tight shut, her hands over her face to hide her embarrassment and stress. As she went to draw another breath, she heard a suppressed giggle, a snort of laughter, coming from Bobe Elka. Anger flared in her, hot and sharp, like red iron. "It's not FUNNY!" she shouted, jumping to her feet and throwing her hands down, whirling towards the elderly witch. And that was when she caught sight of Kurra, frozen, with the bottle of milk to her lips, her eyes flicking from Chi to Elka, to Josephine, and back.

"Reckon as they 'obs is more difficult to get rid of than you think, lass," Bobe Elka managed, between hoots of laughter.

Chidiebere didn't know whether to laugh or cry. The arrival of the hob had flummoxed her. A smile crept into the corners of her mouth. She felt relief, yes, but now more than ever, confusion and a tsunami of questions. She wiped her eyes on her sleeve.

"Kurra, what on earth is going on? And how is it you are here?"

Kurra put the bottle of milk down with what looked like reverence, or maybe reluctance. Wiped her mouth. Turned to Josephine.

"I thank thee, Mistress Josephine, for the milk." She turned back to Chi. "Chidiebere-ma'am, I know not what is 'appening, but I do know that the Pope is not to be trusted, and his men are not to be trusted, and that ... that witch ..." She turned to Josephine. "Beggin' thy pardon, ma'am." Josephine nodded. "That witch, Aedredd the elf, is not to be trusted. She smells of greed and betrayal."

"Aedredd, you say? Aye. She's a rum bugger. Wouldn't trust her with a spoon in a coal shed. Bad news, all round," commented Bobe Elka.

"Who are you, again? You know me mam, you know that ... weird woman, Aedredd ... Hang on." Chi faltered, turned to Kurra. "Did you say *elf*?"

"Sit down, love," said Josephine, her voice gentle, coaxing. She took Chi's arm and guided her back to the chair before the fire. "Here's your tea. Plenty of sugar. Drink up."

"Thanks." Chi sat, then looked up at her, feeling a warmth for the weird hedge witch who had become her friend. Their friend, hers and Kurra's. She glanced at Kurra as she sipped her tea. The hob had picked up the bottle and was polishing it off.

"Reckon you needs to tell the story, now; well, one of you does, or both," suggested Bobe Elka.

"I'll tell you what occurred, for me," began Chidiebere, sipping her tea, trying to relax but failing. "I came into work today and Kurra appeared, like she does, y'know, out of thin air. Only, in the ladies' loo. Which was a first. I was washing my hands. She said ... something ..." Chi screwed her eyes shut, trying to remember. "I dunno. About the Pope? My memory's all fuzzy. I reckon I drank something, but I don't know what. Anyway. I went into Jamie's office – that's my boss, the owner of the factory – and there were these people there ...” She stopped, pushed her glasses up her nose. Buying time. Looked around at the three people watching her. “Um, I’m not making much sense ...”

“It’s OK, love. Carry on as best you can. I think I know what happened, but tell us.”

“I really don’t remember much, it’s like a fog every time I try to think of it. I was pouring water on my coffee, and went to find Kurra, and her home was all gone, where she has ... had, her bed ...”

“I apologise, ma’am, but I cleaned it out, the Pope’s man would’ve found it. Or Aedredd.” Kurra shuddered.

“And what of you, Kurra?” asked Josephine.

“Last night I overheard them talkin’ about pumps and gold. The soldier man spotted me, but I hid in the roof. The Cardinal had an engineer with him. Then this mornin’ I were waiting for Chidiebere to warn her, but the soldier came in, and he was lookin’ for me so I hid in the roof again. I felt Chidiebere come in so I went to warn her because the elf were asking after her. But then the elf found us, in the toilets, so I hid again. I heard Chidiebere-ma’am tell Aedredd that I were in the roof, hidin’. So I ran.” She turned to look at Chi. “Ma’am, I think thou were put under the glamour. I felt it strong, but I managed to run away. I didn’t know what to do so I hid in your conveyance. In the dark smelly compartment with the plumbing tools.”

“You hid in the boot of my car?”

“Aye, ma’am.”

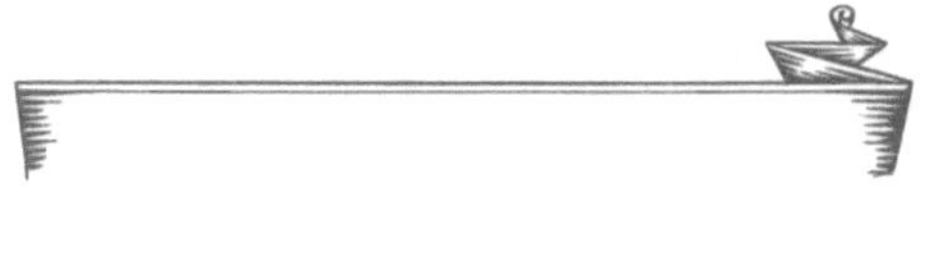

Chapter 11

While Josephine made more tea, Bobe Elka stood with her staff and paced. She tapped the staff on the ground as she went, up and down, over the close-cropped sward. When the tea was ready, she halted by the fire and faced the three of them.

"This bodes badly, I have to say. Tis plain to me, Chi, lass, that you were glamoured to make you say what you said about Kurra. That's why you can't remember the details. The elvish glamour, it fogs your brain an' makes you do stuff you wouldn't otherwise do."

Chi felt a surge of relief. Sort-of relief. She hadn't been drugged. Was coercion through elven magic better or worse than that?

"The question is, though," continued Bobe Elka, "what's the Gratadei up to that they're hangin' around Witcerce? And what's that Aedredd doing, assistin' them?"

"Gratadei?" asked Chi. "What's that?"

"They're essentially the armed wing of the Church. Holy conquistadores appointed by the Pope. With guns." Josephine commented, her tone cutting.

Bobe Elka frowned. "Aye, you can prob'ly tell, we're not fans."

"So what are they after? What do they want with pumps?" Chi was still confused. It was clear to her from the quizzical faces around the fire that everyone else was just as perplexed.

Bobe Elka sipped her tea, then ruminated, "P'raps they are lookin' to take over Khôra, as we suspected they might, years ago. Surprised they've waited this long."

Chidiebere continued to reel with confusion. "Khôra? What's that?"

"Tis a fabled place, Chidiebere-ma'am," said Kurra with a wistful smile. "Where the hobs an' other fae are safe from persecution, an' the fruit is plentiful on the trees, an' the weather is warm all year, an' no one has to clean anything—"

She was interrupted by Bobe Elka, snorting in derision. "You been smoking pipe-weed or summat? Tis not so fabled, an' there's still cleaning to be done. Besides, I thought 'obs liked cleaning?"

Kurra's ears drooped. "It is true, Mistress Elka, I do like things to be clean and free of dust. But is Khôra real, or not? I would dearly like to go there."

"Aye, it's real. Though I think if the Gratadei get their way, it will be a worse place than here in Breotonlond, an' that's saying summat."

"Elka, should we perhaps go to Khôra and warn the Ostiarium that things are afoot?" Josephine suggested, then looked at Chidiebere's furrowed brow. "Sorry. The Ostiarii are the gatekeepers of Khôra. They are elven, but, one hopes, good elves. From Eireann, they are known as Daoine Sidhe, the people of the mounds. Or the Tuatha de Danaan, Danu's people. The Ostiarium is sort of like their governing council."

"Aye, we should," asserted Bobe Elka. She turned to Chi with a grin. "Chidiebere, you 'ave a car? We can go to the gateway this arternoon, if you like?"

Chi's heart fluttered. Elves! A different land? She couldn't quite believe it. She wanted to believe it, but ... "You're pulling my leg, right? Secret land of faeries? Like a kid's book?"

"Nay lass. Much better'n a kiddie's book. But there's not just elves there. All sorts lurkin' in the woodwork. Might be dangerous ..."

"Oh, Chidiebere-ma'am, if we could go." Kurra was hopping from one foot to another, vibrating with excitement. "If we could go, I would be most careful to look to thou an' keep thee safe. I am – I'm sure thou wilt attest – a most resourceful hob, an' diligent!"

Chi laughed. "Very well, hob. We shall go. What the heck, it's not like I'm going back to work any time soon, not with Miss Icy Elf Queen hanging around the place with her hypno-ray."

Chapter 12

Chi led the two Roma witches and Kurra to her car, which sat, forlorn, in the little gravel area at the front of the cottage.

"Just a sec," she called over her shoulder and set about the back seat of the car, excavating the actual seats from a mountain of old crisp packets, magazines, tools, an elderly road atlas, another high-vis coat and a can of screen defroster. She bundled the detritus into the coat and dropped the whole lot into the boot, slamming it, then whirled around and grinned at the three watching friends. "Just pretend you didn't see that, right?"

"Thy storage compartment is now overfull, methinks," muttered Kurra. "Mayst I sit upon a seat instead?"

"Yes, of course, get in. Bobe Elka, perhaps you can be in the front seat to direct me?" With her passengers settled and strapped in, Kurra holding the back of Chi's seat the better to peer about, Chi drove them back towards the main road. "Where are we going, by the way?"

"To the abbey. It's left here, I'll direct you," said Josephine, from the back. Bobe Elka, Chi noticed, had become taciturn upon entering the car, her hands showing white at the knuckles as she gripped the seat's edge. She tried her best to drive in a sedate and careful manner.

The abbey was much as she remembered it from a school trip six years previous. A vast field of grass, dotted with the remains of stone walls, a few solitary pillars, the archway of the old nave on the western end. It dated, she remembered, from before the time of the Tudor kings when the Breotonlond Church fell out with the Pope. She wondered at the idea that the papacy was now ascendant. Was it? She didn't follow politics. Or religious politics, come to that.

There were a couple of tourists looking at an information board at the entrance to the field, but they departed as the company of friends arrived, giving them a sidelong glance but not otherwise engaging them in conversation. Just how Chi liked it.

"Is it in the same place it was before?" asked Josephine.

"Oh aye. You can't move 'em, they go all fizzy and useless," replied Bobe Elka.

"Can't move what?" Chi was confused. Again. It seemed her constant state, today.

"The claves. The keys. Clavis is key in Latin. S'wot they Ostiariuses calls 'em." said Bobe Elka. "They're weird twelve-sided bronze things. Here we are." She waved at a stone wall, between two imposing pillars. There had been a large doorway or gateway in the wall at some point in the past, thought Chi, but it had been filled in and the stone dressed in the same manner as that on either side. "The clavis is in that 'ole in the ground, see?" Bobe Elka pointed at a square of stone set in the ground directly in front of the arched stone doorway. The one that was filled in with stone.

"No, I don't see. You mean there's a bronze twelve-sided key in a hole under the stone?" Chi asked.

"That's right," said Josephine, a breezy smile on her face. "Say the words, Elka."

Bobe Elka drew herself up, then muttered a short phrase in a language Chi didn't recognise. No ceremony. No waving a wand. Nothing, except ...

Where the stone-not-a-doorway had been, a blue-grey meniscus of light came into being. Chi's hair stood on end, her scalp tingling. At the limit of her hearing, she could detect a faint crackle, like electricity discharging from power lines in a storm. Looking at the rippling, iridescent grey surface of the gateway made her eyes go funny.

"Come on. Quick now, before more tourists come," suggested Bobe Elka, and she stepped into the grey surface which swallowed her with hardly a ripple. Chidiebere let out a squeak of alarm.

"Kurra, you next, just walk through. Don't stop or try to turn around. You follow, Chi, I'll bring up the rear." Josephine certainly sounded calm and in charge, thought Chi. Far calmer than she herself felt. She saw Kurra's diminutive frame disappear into the void, then it was her turn. She closed her eyes and stepped forward. The meniscus was clammy, electrostatic, and she experienced a disorientating dizziness and a sliding sensation, as if she was falling.

Strong hands grabbed her arm as she stumbled. She opened her eyes to find Bobe Elka holding her upright, a toothy grin on her face. "First time's allus a bit much on the senses. Walk on, now, make room for Jo."

Chi stepped forward and then stopped once more to look back. Had she just travelled through a wormhole in space-time? They had emerged from a similarly glowing surface on a similar wall, with a stone doorframe; but there were differences. The stone wasn't part of a ruin but built as a simple section of wall, with a portico roof above and a tiny formal garden laid out around it. She peered past the edge of the portico wall to the other side. No abbey ruins. Just shrubbery and a small, neat lawn, studded with fruit trees in blossom. The trees, she noticed, were also in fruit. Apples, peaches, oranges. The weather was clement, and diffuse sunlight warmed her face. They were in a large courtyard with the portico and wall at one end. A long, low, single-storey villa with stucco walls and a pantile roof took up the far end of the area. Against the back wall of the courtyard were lean-to sheds holding, she suspected, livestock and storerooms. A double gate, open to near fields of crops and distant rolling hills, was let into the high walls of the courtyard. The ground was flagged with a warm, biscuit-coloured stone.

She heard Josephine muttering a phrase behind her – she still wasn't able to place the language, and there was a loud pop as if a huge cork had been pulled from a bottle. She turned to see the gateway now gone, and just a stone wall with a doorway set into it. The doorway, as at the abbey, had been filled in with well-pointed stone. She noticed with interest another stone set into the ground, of the same dimensions as that on the other side. Another key, perhaps?

Josephine noticed her stare. "Yes, there's a clavis on each side. Otherwise, you'd only be able to open it from one side. Or not at all."

Chi was intensely curious. "What's the language you used?"

"Old High Romani. But basically, any of the elder languages will do. Ancient Greek. Old Norse. You just need the intention. Open sesame would work if you like. Only, obviously, not that, that's just for kid's theatre."

"Could you teach me?"

"What, let you have the ability to travel between the realms at will, like one of us?"

Chi blushed, utterly embarrassed at her folly for asking. Then realised that Bobe Elka was sniggering, and Josephine was grinning, trying, herself, to suppress the laughter that was bubbling up, irrepressible. "You're closer to being chivani than you might think. Though not a Rom one; has your mum not mentioned her heritage? She has the sight. So too do you. Of course I'll teach you the gateway commands."

Chi smiled, still unsure. "Chivani? That's witch, right?"

"Aye, duck," said Bobe Elka. "We could call you the Plumber Sorcerer, I reckons."

Now Chi blushed fully. She had learnt the spell that Josephine had tried to employ, had tested it and revised it and felt out the strangeness of its form, all without really realising what she was doing. Now, she could stop a leak by invoking the spell, by simply thinking the invoking. It was extremely handy in emergency plumbing call-outs since she could fix pipes and fittings without turning the water off at the mains, making her, she reckoned, the fastest plumber in Witcerce. She was certainly getting a reputation for being competent.

"Chidiebere-ma'am, thou hast the sight, of course, or'se how couldst thou have called me?" Kurra added, bowing to her. Chi blushed even more.

"Salve!" The shout from the steps leading to the villa made them all turn and look; a young man in a simple tunic and sandals stood at the top, one arm raised in greeting.

"Well met, Martin!" Bobe Elka shouted back. "Good to see yer! Come on, you lot. There's bound to be pastries, an' that." Elka leant on her stick and strode over towards the man, Martin, who came down the steps and clasped Bobe Elka's arm, his hand on her forearm, her hand on his. Josephine turned to the other two.

"Come on. Elka's right, there's always pastries and wine," she said, smiling at Martin.

MARTIN SHOWED THE FOUR of them into a reception room. It had a mosaic-tiled floor, plain blue wall hangings over off-white plaster and open beams overhead. An adjoining doorway led, she presumed, to other rooms. There was a low table and an assortment of large cushions made from, Chi realised when she sat on one, a hessian material stuffed with what felt like straw or hay, mixed with feathers. Curious.

She still couldn't quite believe that she, they, had travelled to another realm, as Josephine called it. Where, exactly, were they? Still on Earth? Another planet? A parallel dimension? So many questions. She glanced at Kurra, who was looking in wide-eyed awe at everything around her.

"You OK, Kurra?" she asked, her voice low.

"Chidiebere-ma'am," she replied, her voice similarly hushed, her face shining with wonder. "I canst feel other hobs! I'm not alone! Excepting thyself, ma'am."

"I'm really glad for you, Kurra. That's great news. I hope you get to speak with them, meet them, soon." Chi was smiling as well.

Martin returned carrying a tray laden with food; a steaming jug of some sort of mulled wine, by the smell, thought Chi. And tiny delicate pastries that were glazed, glossy and hot.

As Martin poured drinks for them, and they helped themselves to the pastries, a tall, androgynous woman walked in through the adjoining doorway. Chidiebere tried not to stare. The woman had pointed ears peeking out through her long straight white hair. An actual elf, she thought.

"Kushti divvus, mistresses Elka and Josephine. It is good to see you again," said the elf, her voice soft, sibilant. Bobe Elka raised her glass of hot wine, still chewing on a pastry, flecks on her lips. Josephine merely nodded at the elf and introduced the others.

"Hello again, Ostiarius. Please allow me to introduce Plumber Sorcerer Chidiebere of Witcerce, daughter of Obi Adebayo, and Kurra of Cazmielou, daughter of Kochonitze." She turned to Kurra and Chi. "This is Ostiarius Aelene de Danaan, keeper of the Witcerce gateway."

"Though in truth," said the tall elf with a smile, "there is little enough traffic that it hardly needs keeping."

As Aelene chatted with the two Roma witches, whom Chi presumed she was familiar with as they talked of past events and future plans, she watched the interactions of the people. Martin was deferential, observant, standing by the door.

Josephine was in an animated discussion with Aelene about whether it would be possible to move the gateway from the ruined abbey. Bobe Elka, Chi saw, was also watching. Watching Aelene, a contemplative look upon her face. Kurra was similarly observing Aelene, and her face was not contemplative but bordering on hostile.

"Kurra? What's wrong?" Chi asked in a quiet tone, almost a whisper, leaning close to Kurra's ear.

"I shalt tell thou later, Chidiebere-ma'am," she replied, formally. At the same time, Bobe Elka stood up and tapped her staff on the floor, bringing everyone's attention to her.

"Now then. The thing about it is, like. Chidiebere here has summat to say." She waved her staff at Chi.

"I do?" She was surprised. Then realised, it was her story to tell. "Oh, yes, I do. Um." She also stood up and faced Aelene, who seated herself at the table on a cushion, all the while looking intently at Chi.

Chi took a breath, steadied her nerves, and began her tale, from when she spun the spell to summon Kurra.

"... AND SO WE DECIDED to come here to warn you," Chidiebere finished. The telling of the tale had taken all afternoon, with interruptions from Aelene, and additions from Bobe Elka and Josephine. Kurra, Chi noticed, had stayed very quiet and withdrawn throughout. What on earth was wrong with her? Chi sat down on the cushion and took a sip of her drink.

Aelene stood and bowed to them.

"I thank you all for attending today and imparting your thoughts and worries. I can only assure you that we are aware of the Gratadei's plans and have put countermeasures in place." She looked at each of them with a smile on her face. Chi felt the stirrings of something fearful. Her smile didn't reach her eyes. Kurra was right – something about this Ostiarius was off. "Now, if you will excuse me, I have other business to attend to." She swept from the room, her cream silk robes rustling as she glided away.

"Um ..." started Chi.

"Best be away, an' all!" exclaimed Bobe Elka, snagging the remaining few pastries and clambering to her feet. "Gorra see a man about a dog. Come on, let's 'ave a chat at the gateway." She nodded her head towards the door. Her face looked serious, and Chi felt fear tingling her scalp.

They trooped out, Elka, Kurra, Chi and Josephine bringing up the rear. Martin hovered by the door. As Bobe Elka passed Martin, she must have said something because his countenance darkened as well and he gave an almost imperceptible nod.

At the gateway portico, now just so much stonework, they regrouped.

"Summat's afoot, sure as eggs is tiny chickens," muttered Bobe Elka, when they had all arrived at the portico. "Aelene's acting right funny. Dunno what's up with 'er but summat is."

"I am in agreement," said Kurra. "There is somethin' that makes me worry we have brought our tale to the wrong person." Her voice was low and even, her manner formal and tight.

"Her smile didn't reach her eyes," added Chi, pursing her lips in disapproval. Then she stopped, catching herself. Her mam's mannerisms, trickling through. She rolled her eyes at herself, internally.

Martin approached. Josephine turned to him. "Martin, well met. You've been Aelene's helper here for some time? Is there something wrong that she isn't telling us about?"

He bowed to the four of them. Smiling, but with no humour, he let out a sigh. "She is under a lot of stress. Rosalia, the Ostiarius Principale, is talking of shutting the gateways down, to prevent the Gratadei from gaining a foothold in Khôra. Obviously, Aelene and many other Ostiarii do not want to shut them down. It would have serious repercussions on the economy of the land, such as it is."

"Well, I can see that would make her a bit stressed. But what other defences do you have against the Gratadei?"

He bowed his head. "My Ladies, I regret that I am in no position to discuss the politics and tribulations within the Ostiarium."

"That's alright, duck, we can see the message on the wall, like. Ta all the same." Bobe Elka patted Martin on the arm, then turned to Josephine. "Best you take these two back to Witcerce, an' I'll travel by yog up to the north an' see if I can get an inside line on what's happening, like. Might take some time."

Josephine didn't look overly pleased with this plan, that much was plain to Chidiebere.

"We can make our own way back if you need to stay here, Josephine," she said.

Josephine frowned, deep in thought. Then her face brightened. "No, Bobe Elka is right, we'll go back together. Now, Elka, you'll send word the moment you have something?

These two, at least, have a right to know, them bein' embroiled in all this."

"Aye, don't you fret, lasses. I'll be in touch. Kushti bok!" Bobe Elka turned and, with a wave of her hand, marched away, towards the open gateway that led to the rolling countryside beyond.

Chi felt suddenly exposed, just the three of them, in the gloaming of the evening. A chill wind had arrived, teasing at the edges of her clothes, finding its way in through unwary seams. She shivered.

"We'll get back shortly," said Josephine, turning to Chi, "but I think you need to learn the words. Ah, do you know the language of your mother? That might work well."

Chi was confused. Again. There was still cotton wool fluffing up her brain. "You mean Igbo? Yes, I know it."

"So, you need a phrase that is clear in its intention, and comes from the heart, to open the gateway."

"Like 'Open Sesame', but in Igbo?"

"Yes. like that. But not that. And feel the words as well. Believe them. Direct them at the gateway."

"Um. How about, er ..." She closed her eyes, thinking the words. Felt a weird stirring in her heart. Opened her eyes, looked at the blank stone of the portico. Here goes nothing. "*Ana m enye gi iwu imeghe!*" She delivered it in a direct tone – even and, she hoped, commanding. Her hair stood on end as an odd feeling washed over her, and the blue-grey meniscus of the gateway snapped into place with a barely audible crackle. "Oh my fucking God!" she squeaked. Clapping her hand over her mouth, she glanced down at Kurra. But the hob, and Josephine were both grinning.

"I told thee, thou hast the sight, Chidiebere-ma'am," declared Kurra.

"You do indeed," remarked Josephine. "Now, try the same sort of words, but for closing. Think them from the heart. Say them to the gateway."

Again, Chidiebere thought, composed herself, and again felt the tingling in her chest. "*Ana m enye gị iwu ka ị nọrọ na emechi!*" No sooner were the words from her mouth, than with a gentle pop the meniscus disappeared. She turned to Josephine. "How does it do that?"

"Well. No one really knows. They were built by Hephaestus, smith to the Athenian gods, and his descendants. All we know is that if you move the claves, they don't open a gateway. Without a clavis, the gateway is not openable. The claves have to be in the right place. Come on, I could use a cuppa." She muttered her own words and the meniscus reappeared. "You first, Chi, then Kurra. I'll follow on."

With a final look around the darkened garden and yard, with Martin shutting the gates for the night, Chi stepped through the gateway and back to Witcerce Abbey.

"BEFORE WE GO, CHI, Kurra ..." Josephine began.

Chidiebere turned around on the grass next to the now ordinary stone-filled doorway. "Yes?" Curiosity picked at her, but also exhaustion.

"Ma'am?" added Kurra.

"I'm not suggesting anything, but ... under that stone" – she waved her foot at the flat light brown stone set in the grass – "is a clavis. Same on the other side. You can't open a gateway without a clavis on the same side. I don't recommend any course of action that would annoy the Ostiarium, but on the other hand, you never know when having control of a gateway might give you an advantage. Of course, you never heard that from me ..." She grinned. "Shall we go have that cup of tea?"

Chapter 13

Kurra stood on the folded coat, pulled the seat belt across her chest, and, still holding it, sat and clipped it in. She wasn't sure why she needed to be belted into the seat, but Chidiebere-ma'am had said it was the law, and she felt it was probably best to at least try to obey the laws of her kyrios. *Trying to make amends for past failures,* slithered the snide voice at the back of her mind. *You can't make amends for everything. No matter how many rules you now obey,* it whispered.

"Shu' up. Thou dun't know nuffin."

"What's that?" Chi asked as she got in the car.

"I am talking to myself, Chidiebere-ma'am," Kurra mumbled.

"Well. Where would you like to go? I'm guessing not to the factory. You can come home with me?"

"Chidiebere-ma'am, I know not what to do. If I go to the factory, the soldier may come and find me. Or the elf." She shuddered. "But if I come to thine abode, then they may come there also."

"Do you really think they'll start looking for us if we just stay out of their way?"

"I know not. I am worried. For thou. And for me."

"Well. It's late. We'll go to my house, well, me mam's house, and then see what tomorrow brings. OK?"

"If thou wishes, ma'am," said Kurra, a heaviness in her voice. She felt a great fear rising in her. The whispering, insidious, started again. *Thou shalt bring ruin on her home, Kurra of Cazmielou …*

KURRA SETTLED ON A stool in the small kitchen in Mistress Obi's house. She looked around, appraising the furnishings. It appeared very clean. She tried to relax, but her body seemed to be vibrating with tension, fear.

"Milk? I think there's fresh," asked Chi, pulling open the fridge.

"Yes please, Chidiebere-ma'am. Milk is always welcome."

"Is that you, Chi?" A shout came from the hallway as the front door slammed shut. "Are you just back from the factory now? You are working too hard!" A tall, well-built woman with long black braids looped into a topknot bustled into the kitchen carrying a pair of woven shopping bags bursting with vegetables. "And who is this hobgoblin you have brought into the house?"

"Hi, mam. This is—"

"Is it house-trained? I will not have it in the house if it makes a mess!"

"Mam … this is—"

"Do not interrupt me! Who are you, hobgoblin? Do you speak?"

Kurra had been flicking her eyes from Chi to her mother and back, keeping otherwise utterly still. She took a breath and spoke before Obi could continue.

"Good evening, Mistress Obi. My name is Kurra. I thank thee for the hospitality of thy clean home. I am ... house-trained, aye, and I will not make a mess. I am a helpful, cleaning hob."

Obi turned to Chi. "Is this the hobgoblin you tell me about from the factory? I thought you were makin' stories again, taking your grandmam's book an' doing that *anwansi*."

"Yes mam, this is that hobgoblin. And you do *anwansi* all the time!"

"Hmph!" Obi set the shopping down on the work surface with a thump. "And what are you doin' here, hobgoblin? Why are you not at the factory?" She turned to Chi, who was biting her lower lip. "What has happened? I can tell, you know. Something has happened." She fixed them both with her stare, sucked her teeth. Chidiebere flinched. Mam meant business. "You will not leave this kitchen until you tell me!"

Chapter 14

"I'm really not sure this is a good idea," Chidiebere said, as she pulled her car into a parking space in the next industrial unit along from the factory. The small stream and the undergrowth separated the two plots. Kurra stood on the front seat and peered through the side window at the tarmac, the undergrowth, the stream, the undergrowth, the path, the fire door. "And how are you gonna get in through the fire door? Do you have lock-picking skills or burglary experience? Actually, I'm not sure I want to know ..."

"Chidiebere-ma'am, I will be alright. I am able to do it. I am a hob." It was almost a lie by omission. Almost. Before Chidiebere could change her mind, Kurra leant into slow time and slipped from the vehicle. She walked around to the boot and gently, oh so gently, lifted the lid, reached inside, fetched a crowbar, and shut the boot again. She walked through the undergrowth, jumped the stream, and arrived at the fire door.

She used the crowbar the way any common burglar, or firefighter, would. Inserting the curved end into the space between the doors, she used the leverage afforded by the tool's length to force the doors slightly apart, until the latch clicked out and the door opened. She smiled to herself, ducked inside, shut the door again.

Kurra made her way to the main factory space. The day was yet early, the sun had hardly risen; no cars were in the car park, and she expected no one to be in the factory itself. She climbed up to her previous vantage point above the main part of the building but found herself a more comfortable and more hidden alcove, between the structural beam supporting the roof and the skin of the roof itself. Even with the lights off, she was confident that no one could see her from below.

"HOW WAS IT?" CHIDIEBERE asked, as Kurra climbed back into the car at the end of the day.

"There is nothing to report, Chidiebere-ma'am. The workers build normal pumps. None of the Cardinal's company were present. Master Britten spent most of the day in his office. I did not clean."

"You don't have to clean. You know that, right?"

"I know it, ma'am. But I like cleaning!" Kurra's eyes shone.

"So … I've been meaning to talk to you about something," Chi began, her tone tentative.

Kurra felt a prickle of fear. "What is it, Chidiebere-ma'am?"

"You're bound to me. Because of the spell. And the milk."

"Aye, that is so."

"How do you feel about that?"

Kurra was silent for a few moments. How did she feel? She longed for release from the cycle of servitude, only because her previous masters and mistresses had been so cruel, or their circumstances grindingly dismal. She didn't want to not serve Chidiebere. She liked her kyrios. But at the same time, she wasn't unaware of Chidiebere's heritage. And the terrible state of millions of enslaved people. She had seen enough in her various and varied services to know of the plight of people of all skin colour, enslaved or worse.

"I will speak plainly, ma'am, though it be difficult for me. For a long time, I have tried to break my cycle of servitude, not because I do not wish to serve, but because I wish to do more with my life. Other hobs would say I am an aberration, to wish this. But that is my character. I ... I have done questionable things in my life. Things that fall outside the hob lore. Breaking away from servitude would also be outside the hob lore. But I do not wish to *not* serve *thee*. Thou art a most generous and kind kyrios." She looked up at Chi's face. She plunged on. "I know that in this time there are few enslaved people, at least not like in previous eras, and not so much in Breotonlond. But I can see that this is a problem for you, because of your heritage." She looked into Chi's eyes. Put her hand on Chi's arm. "I ... I am most fond of you, Chidiebere-ma'am. I wish to serve you, but also to be your friend."

She could see Chi was embarrassed. A flush darkened her skin, and she was fidgeting as she did when she was troubled.

"I am sorry, ma'am, I do not wish to cause thee distress."

Chi fumbled for a tissue from the box between the front seats and blew her nose, dabbed her eyes. "Oh, Kurra," she said, her voice cracking with emotion. "You don't cause me distress. You're amazing, and kind, and sensible, and I really like you. Come on, let's get home. I bet you're starving. Mam's making jollof and chicken." Chi started the engine and drove out of the parking lot.

"Would there be more of the condensed milk?" Kurra enquired. The thought of another tin of the amazing, rich, tasty milk made her stomach flutter.

"You're impossible! And it makes you go all funny!" Chi laughed, shaking her head.

KURRA WAS HAPPY WITH the routine. Chi would drop her off in the morning, she would watch from her hiding place, and Chi would collect her in the evening. It had a certain gentle monotony about it that soothed her soul. The factory workers were building pumps for ships, for the Fenland irrigations, for, well, anything. But not something mysterious. There had been no sign of the new different pump, or the Cardinal and his cohort. For over a week. But all that had changed today.

"So? How did it go?" Chi asked, as Kurra slipped back into real time in Chidiebere's car, as the sun set at the end of the day.

"Today the engineer who was with the Cardinal came and spoke to the men, and measured things, and checked drawings. He seemed satisfied, and he left again. Master Britten also came to look at the new machine they are building. I overheard the men talking about the mystery of what it will pump and where it will be installed. They are taking bets on which of them will be on the installation team. They think it will be in Araby or the East Indies."

"So they are going ahead with the construction?"

"Yes, that is the case."

Chapter 15

Kurra skipped over the stream, the water silent, unmoving, as if it were frozen in midwinter. Pushed through the undergrowth, smelt the phlox flowers in passing. Arrived at the fire door. Edged the crowbar into the gap, now well-worn and obvious, but only if you looked for it. Opened the door with silence and ease. Slid inside. Closed the door behind her. Took a step into the gloom of the corridor.

The binding was instant, tightening about her torso and arms as if a python had her. She plummeted out of slow time like a shot game bird, both physically and chronologically, with a thump that jarred her spine. She could not move; fear cascaded into her mind, thoughts whirling. Her skin sweated and prickled, terror and elven magic coruscating over her in equal measure. Materialising from a concealing glamour before her was Aedredd, tall and haughty and looking very pleased with herself.

"It seems I have caught a hobgoblin," she said. "A sneaking, thieving, spying hobgoblin. Tell me, how does it sit with the hob lore to be here like this? Breaking into your kyrios' employer's building?"

Kurra did not speak. She needed to free herself from these invisible bonds. She could not move, physically. She reached for slow time, but ... couldn't find it! As if part of her soul had been excised. She trembled, claws of fear raking her guts.

"Oh, what's that? Can't find your ability to change time? You'd still be trapped by my enchantments, even then."

Enchantments? Then she saw them. Dishes of a grey-black liquid, set about the edges of the corridor. A line of small white crystals, like poured rock salt, delineated a circle which surrounded Kurra. Black candles, guttering things, punctuated the salt line at intervals. The smoke was cloying and acrid. Oh, this was very bad. This looked like some sort of human magic that the elf had subverted. A hybrid.

"What, cat got your tongue? Well. Here's what will happen. You need to stop spying. Which means, you need to die. Or be returned to your sleep. Which means your kyrios must die. Which is it to be, hobgoblin? You, or your blackamoor girlfriend?"

Kurra's head spun. Why didn't Aedredd just kill her now? She was bound by magic, couldn't move, couldn't dodge a knife or a club. Why threaten Chidiebere? Something didn't make sense. Then she had it. Aedredd was outside the circle. She couldn't come into the circle. So Kurra was trapped, but safe. As safe as being immobilised within the presence of a deranged elf allowed, at least.

"I couldn't care less about the kyrios. Kill her an' let me sleep," she said, hoping to goad, or buy time, or ... something.

She heard a door open beyond Aedredd in the corridor, and footsteps approached. Hope flared that they would be disturbed, allowing her to escape. Her hope withered and died as the soldier of the New God arrived, holding something black and reminiscent of a flintlock pistol, the last firearm Kurra had seen.

"You're late." Aedredd's voice softened as she turned to the soldier, who smiled at her, shrugging, as if to say, "I'm here now."

"Shoot the hob," ordered Aedredd, pointing at Kurra.

Kurra's mind raced. So this was their plan. She couldn't slow time, wouldn't be able to dodge the bullet. Even if she *could* slow time, she was held fast, immobile. As the soldier raised his weapon and sighted at Kurra, bringing his other hand up to steady the pistol and taking a wide stance on the balls of his feet, Kurra reached inside herself, to her place between. She grasped it with her mind, her very soul. And pulled. She mentally and physically wrenched herself to her between place, feeling the elven magic slipping, writhing, losing purchase. With a snap it gave way, and she flew into her place, breath steaming from the cold. She disappeared from the world, and all about her was grey and cold and mist. The monotony was only broken by her store of candles, forlorn on the grey ground. She could already feel the strength leaving her limbs. She couldn't stay here long; the magic of the binding to Chidiebere pulled at her. But she could come back to the world in her own direction. She took two steps, then another, and allowed herself to be sucked back into the living world. She was in the corridor, behind Aedredd. Behind the soldier. And beyond the enchantments. She immediately pushed into slow time.

The soldier was still holding the gun, smoke darkening the air in front of it, a fresh hole in the fire door letting in a beam of sunlight. Aedredd was turning, as if through treacle, but still, impossibly fast. Kurra felt the drag on her own magic – Aedredd was pulling herself into the slow time! Without thinking, Kurra raised the crowbar, jumped into the air with her slow time strength and agility, and struck at Aedredd's head. The crowbar caught her on the forehead, a glancing blow, but enough to split the elf's skin from brow to crown, snapping her head back. Kurra felt the elven magic snuff out, and Aedredd returned to her own temporal flow, standing, blood floating in almost stationary droplets in a line from the cut, and away towards the ceiling. Kurra landed, still clutching the now bloodied crowbar, panting from the exertion. She turned and ran.

Through her panic, she tried to formulate a plan, rather than fleeing, oblivious to further danger. Though by now she was at the front of the factory. She scanned constantly for more traps, more enchantments. None were obvious. She arrived at the main door, saw it was ajar, sunlight spilling in from outside. She sprinted, bursting into the car park and away into the undergrowth and bushes on the far side. She still didn't slow down. Distance. And find Chidiebere, warn her. These were her priorities. She could feel the reservoir of slow time emptying with her exertions.

How long had it been since she left Chidiebere? Thirty seconds? A minute? She couldn't have driven far. She scanned the street as she ran. There! The battered blue car, just turning into the road towards the factory from the car park next door, but crawling, slow time allowing Kurra to catch it up. She opened the passenger door, slipped inside, closed it, fastened her seat belt. Dropped into real time.

"What the fuck?" exclaimed Chidiebere.

"Keep going! The elf almost caught me. The soldier tried to shoot me."

"What? Shit, you're covered in blood!"

"Keep going. I am unharmed."

"Shit. OK." The car wobbled as Chi grasped for composure. "Whose blood is it?"

"The elf. I think I slowed her d— Oh no. Do not stop, Chidiebere-ma'am," Kurra implored. A figure had appeared at the entrance to the factory. The soldier. He raised the gun, took aim. Aedredd, blood pouring down her face, also stepped from the door and pushed the soldier's arm down. Kurra could see her mouthing furious words.

"Oh my God, he's got a gun!" Chidiebere screamed, and the car lurched forward, the engine racing. "Kurra, look out the back window, are they following us?"

Kurra turned, watched, her heart hammering in her diminutive chest. As they rounded a corner, she glimpsed the soldier and the elf climbing into a large black car.

"Yes, Chidiebere-ma'am, they are followin' us."

"Shit, shit-shit-shit!" Chi thumped the steering wheel. "What are we going to do? They'll catch us. Will they shoot us? What should we do? Kurra?"

"Be quiet for a moment, please, ma'am," said Kurra, aware as she said it that it was the first time she had asked anything of any kyrios. It felt strangely liberating. She had an idea. She closed her eyes and concentrated on the slow time, and how it was she engaged with it, and how she always moved through slow time in her ragged clothes. Her clothes were not part of her, and yet, they came with her. How? She reached, felt, explored. Pushed, harder than usual, but in an inexplicable, ineffable way, also broader. She opened her eyes. The car was still moving. Though nothing else was.

"What? What the fuck?" Chidiebere was looking around at the other cars, all of which had stopped, or so it seemed. She had to drive around them. The oncoming cars were also stopped. Pedestrians – a pair of children walking to school, their hair frozen in the wind, their chattering faces immobilised. A workman leaning on a shovel by the side of the road, smoking a cigarette, the smoke curling, a still life, his hand grasping the cigarette, unmoving. "You've actually fucking stopped time? I'm sorry for swearing, but. Oh. My. Fucking. God." Chidiebere was grinning now, driving with caution around the stationary traffic. At a junction, she bumped up a kerb to go around the waiting vehicles.

Sweat was beading Kurra's face. "I will not be able to do this for many more seconds, ma'am." Her voice was strained. It was difficult to talk, as if a great weight was inside her chest, trying to get out. "Try to get to a place where the elf will not think to look."

"OK, hang on, I know a route around the town and out that goes ... oh, one-way system! I've always wanted to do this!" Chidiebere giggled as she drove into a narrow street fronted with a circular red and white sign. Again, they drove along the kerb to avoid some vehicles, but then came to a large junction and headed off on a wider road.

"I am going to move us back into the real, ma'am, please be ready," Kurra gasped, and let go of the slow time with a sigh, collapsing onto the seat in a rag-doll heap. Chi squeaked as the traffic around her started moving. A van driver honked his horn as he almost ran into Chi's car from behind, and she accelerated away, waving apologies.

"We've lost them for now … but where should we go? What should we do? Kurra? You OK?" Concern tinged Chi's voice.

Kurra struggled to sit upright, gripping the seat edge. "I am alright, I think, thank thee, ma'am, just a bit tired. I know not where to go. Wherever we go, we may bring the wrath of the Gratadei upon us."

"Well, how about we take this to the Ostiarium? I'm going to the abbey."

"To Khôra, Chidiebere-ma'am?"

"Yep. To Khôra."

Chapter 16

Chi wasn't sure about anything anymore. As if in a surreal dream, she navigated her old car to the ruined abbey. Kurra sat on her pile of high-vis clothes, apparently asleep. As she pulled into the gravel parking area next to the abbey's field entrance, the crunch of their tyres on stone and the jolt of the uneven ground woke the small hobgoblin, who started as if from a deep sleep. She looked around in momentary confusion before seeming to gather her wits again.

"I was dreaming we had escaped, only to be captured on the far side of the gateway," she muttered.

"Well, let's hope that doesn't happen. Come on." As Chi opened the door, a large black sedan approached along the narrow lane, cresting the rise in the road a distance away. "Oh come on! You have got to be kidding me! Think we might need to worry about capture on this side, first!"

"Run, Chidiebere-ma'am! Run!" Kurra shouted, as she jumped down from the car and headed through the field gate, towards the transept archway and the gateway. Chi didn't need any encouragement. Grabbing the keys and her day-bag rucksack, she sprinted after the small figure of Kurra. She could hear the sedan approaching, its engine note high, its tyres chirping complaints. Kurra disappeared.

"Kurra!" she shouted. "Shit. No time. Keep going, Chi." She was the first to admit she preferred a stroll to a sprint, a meat pie or curried lamb to a salad. She was sweating! Breath rasping, limbs shaking, she arrived at the archway that should contain the gateway. No sign of Kurra. Time was running out; the sedan was pulling up behind her car, blocking it in. She shouted the spell, in Igbo, to open the portal. To her considerable relief, it flickered into existence. A second later, Kurra also materialised, or so it seemed. Her hands were covered in soil, and in one she held the crowbar. In the other …

"No way! Kurra! Genius!" she smiled. Kurra was holding a dodecahedron, about the size of an apple, its bronze metal age-dulled and pitted with corrosion. A blue glow emanated from within its hollow centre, visible through holes in its faces.

A shot rang out, a chunk of stone near them pinged and the bullet ricocheted with a whine.

"Shit!" Without thinking, Chi grabbed Kurra up into her arms – crowbar, dodecahedron and all – and hurled herself through the gateway. She landed on her side, on the ornamental lawn of the Ostiarius' villa in Khôra. A bullet cut the air over their heads, hitting the wall of the villa and spanging away. Quick as thought, she cast the closing spell, and the gateway popped out of existence. The dodecahedron in Kurra's hand dulled, the blue glow faded.

"Best hide that, I think. Here, put it in the bag," she said in a guarded tone, looking around from her prone position. Kurra slipped the object into the day bag and Chi pulled the drawstring tight. As she looked up, she saw Kurra flickering back from … somewhere? Then footsteps. She whirled.

Martin loomed over them. "Mistress Chidiebere Adebayo. Hob Kurra. How may I assist you?"

Chi sat up, then stood, having regained her breath to a certain extent at least. She brushed mud from her knees. "Hello, Martin. I wonder, is the Ostiarius here?"

"No, My Lady, matters of state keep her away in Defaltum Mundi."

"De-Defaltum Mundi?"

"That plane of existence from which you have just travelled," he said with a smile, indicating the closed gateway stone behind her. Chi really hoped he hadn't noticed the dodecahedron. Clavis. Thing. He didn't look like he had, at least. And there was no way to check it was missing on the far side of the gateway without going there. She relaxed. Just a little.

"Um. So, I really need to speak with the Ostiarium. How ... how would I go about that?" she asked, her brow furrowed as she tried to calculate how much to trust Martin. She remembered the terse words exchanged between him and Bobe Elka. She felt he was an ally. But she just didn't know. And she was prepared to trust her gut over anything else, just at the present time.

Martin gave her an appraising look. "Your best option, I would suggest, is to make your way to Mediolanum and seek out the Ostiarius Principale Rosalia. She is wise and will offer you just counsel."

"Um. OK. Mediolanum? How far is that? Is there a bus?"

Martin smiled again. "Come into the villa. I will have Cook make you a travel parcel, and you may have a meal before you depart. The purpose of the Ostiarium is, after all, to support gateway travellers. Mediolanum is but a few miles, though the terrain is hilly in places. Half a day's easy walk. As for an omnibus, I am afraid we don't have anything like that in Khôra. You might hitch a ride on a dray if you are passed by one on the road."

"Hitch a ride on a dray? Like a cart?" It was like her world was being pulled from under her.

"Yes, My Lady. Please, come and have a drink, some food."

"Hang on. Let me think, please." She knelt down next to Kurra, who was regarding her and Martin with impatience. Chi's mind was awhirl with thoughts, strategies, what-ifs. What if there was another gateway nearby that Aedredd could access? What if she tracked Kurra and her down on the road? What if Martin was colluding with her? No, that was a step too far. He seemed genuine, and Bobe Elka seemed to approve of him. "What do you think, Kurra?"

"I think we should be away from here and hidden as soon as we possibly can, Chidiebere-ma'am. That is what I think."

"Very well." Her own gut said the same, so that was the decision made. She stood up again, turned to Martin. "I thank you for your hospitality, Martin, but we are in a hurry. Events are ... moving quickly in Defaltum Mundi, and I fear if we stay here we will bring problems for you. If you have a map of how to get to Mediolanum, even a sketch, that would be a great help. But we must be away in the next few minutes."

"Very well. I shall fetch a map." And Martin turned to go.

"Oh! Sorry, Martin, I wonder ... where is the next nearest gateway?"

Martin turned back, the hint of a wry smile on his lips. "The next nearest is at Wayland, My Lady. A mile in that direction." He pointed over Chi's shoulder. "Though in Defaltum Mundi, Witcerce to Wayland is almost one hundred and forty miles. Which is a barrier to travel, if you are seeking to evade people in Witcerce." He glanced at the day bag, and his smile broadened. He turned back to the villa.

Chi's thoughts raced. So he did know they had the Witcerce Abbey clavis in her bag. Well, she was keeping hold of that, for now. And how could it be that the gateway here was close, but hundreds of miles otherwise? Her brain boggled.

Kurra looked up at her. "Art thou ready for a walk, then, Chidiebere-ma'am? If I may be so bold, I would suggest we leave here an' then take a dog leg so as to be off the beaten track an' away in the woods, if they have such things ..." She inhaled through her nose. The air did smell fragrant, thought Chi. The blossom from the fruit trees, she supposed. "I do love the woods. It has been many years since I was able to walk in them." Kurra had a wistful, faraway look on her face.

"YOU KNOW," BEGAN CHI, "now that you're in Khôra, you don't need to be bound to me. I can break the spell. If I did that, would you go back to sleep, or does it work differently here?"

Kurra stopped walking, took a moment, looked out over the wide grassy plain to their right, the rolling wooded hills on their left, the sunlight diffuse, casting a golden, almost magical hue over the land. Insects buzzed lazily in the blossoms lining the path, which rose from the roadway up into the distant foothills.

"If thou were to die, Chidiebere-ma'am, I would be sent back to my between place, to sleep until I am called anew. If thou were to release me, I think I would remain in this world, aye."

Chi could tell that Kurra was excited at the prospect, her heart's desire, after a life – lives – of servitude. "How can I release you?"

Kurra looked up at her, her eyes misted with tears. "'Tis but a simple matter. Thou hast to offer me a gift of worth, somethin' of significance to thee. And I hast to accept it. It must be, as it is said, a gift freely given, with no expectation of reward."

Chi knelt down next to the hob and pulled her day bag from her back, undid the drawstrings, reached inside. Kurra's eyes went wide, and she became very still. Chi pulled the clavis out of the bag and handed it to Kurra.

"A gift, freely given. An item of significant worth to me. I release you from the bindings holding you in my service, Kurra of Cazmielou, daughter of Kochonitze."

Kurra dropped to one knee and bowed her head. She held still, then slowly straightened. Tears were rolling down her weather-beaten face and dripping onto the dusty ground. She took the clavis, grasping it in both hands, and held it to her breast. A shudder ran through her. "I can feel it," she murmured. "It is as if I weigh nothing. I am free. Chidiebere-ma'am, I am free!"

"You can call me Chi, now, right?"

A grin spread over the hob's face. "Aye, I can. It may take me some time to get used to that, however."

Chapter 17

The path they followed levelled out along an escarpment, the far shoulder of which was heavily wooded. The tree line was dense and dark, and Chi was happy that they were not entering its dim cover.

"We should have taken Martin up on his offer of food," suggested Chi. "I'm starving." She scanned the far horizon. Fields and rolling hills, the distance hazed with mist. The day was almost spent, the sun approaching the horizon. "How much further to Mediolanum, do you think?"

"I know not, Chidiebere-ma—" Kurra corrected herself. "Chi. The map is poorly sketched and has no scale. Though, there is food, see?" She reached into the dense foliage at the path side and held up a briar. Its underside was laden with ripe raspberries, their colours deepening from bright red through to a deep burgundy. Then she turned to a stand of tall thin trees, and leapt, grabbing a branch and bending it down, like a bow. The leaves hid tufted nut pods, which she pulled off and shelled. "Hazelnuts." She popped a nut into her mouth, chewed with appreciation. "They are just ripe. It seems it would be impossible to starve in this land, ma'am ... um, Chi."

The next few minutes were punctuated with the sounds of chewing and the swish of bent hazel stands returning to their upright position. Chi wiped raspberry juice from her chin. "Mmm. S'good," she mumbled through a mouth full of berries. She swallowed. "Not sure if I could manage this full-time, though."

"I think I could," replied Kurra, her tone thoughtful. "I could quite easily live in the woods and never come out again."

"Like a hermit?" Chi giggled.

"It is not a laughing matter. I wish for solitude. I cannot explain it."

"Oh. Well. You're a free hob, now. You can do as you wish." Chi felt a pang. If Kurra left, she would sorely miss her. And she would be all on her own in Khôra.

As if reading her thoughts, Kurra said, "I will travel with thee to Mediolanum, Chi. But there I shall leave thee, an' make my own way in the world. It will be … strange, I think. An' I will miss thee. But as thou sayst, I am a free hob, now."

THE LAST OF THE LIGHT was fleeing the day when they crested a pass nestling between two hills. The plain beyond held a smudge of light in the distance. At the top of the rise on the left was a small clearing in the trees, and pulled up on the clearing were a pair of horse-drawn wagons of the same type as Josephine's. A campfire burnt in a rough hearth of stones between them, casting shadows and the silhouettes of seated figures. A dark-coloured dog, indistinct in the gloom, put up a volley of barks before being shushed by one of the figures, who stood.

"Quiet now, Ailesh," came the man's voice. Then louder, "Who's that?"

"Tis Chidiebere Adebayo, Plumber Sorcerer, if I ain't mistook. An' the hob, Kurra." came the familiar Lincoliscire brogue.

"Bobe Elka!" called Chi, walking toward the fire. "I am so glad to find someone I know!" She stopped when the dog let out a warning growl. The man had his hand on the dog's collar.

"Dun't mind 'er, lass, she's all spit an' no spite. Here, have a seat. Cup of tea?" the traveller said. He was tall and skinny and, thought Chi, quite old. Balding with wisps of grey hair which failed to cover enormous ears. He was dressed in old-fashioned trousers, shirt and waistcoat, with a colourful cotton scarf knotted around his neck.

"I'm George. Y'know Elka. This 'ere is Shireen." He waved his hand at a slender woman with dark skin and long straight grey hair, a decorative scarf covering her head. The woman held up her cup, saluting Chi. "An' the dog's Ailesh McCaffrey."

"Hello!" said Chi, slightly out of breath from the climb to the col. "I'm Chi, and this is Kurra ... um ... somewhere ..." She looked around in the encroaching gloom, but Kurra had melted away. Shy? Chi didn't know. She was, after all, a free hob. Another pang went through her, but she rallied as George passed her a cup of steaming hot tea that smelt of home. Ordinary Breotonlond tea. She sipped it and sighed.

The traveller fetched a folding chair from the back of his wagon for Chi, then seated himself back on an upturned wooden crate. Ailesh the dog took her time to lower herself, stiff, Chi guessed, from arthritis; she ended up lying on her side, her paws almost in the embers of the fire. Chi sat on the folding chair.

"Well met, Chi," began Bobe Elka. "What news from Defaltum Mundi?"

Chi's mind whirled. Where to begin? "Well ..." she started.

"... SO KURRA USED HOB time or whatever it is to steal the clavis at the abbey, which is how we managed to evade Aedredd. Martin seemed to understand, I think he knew we had the clavis in the bag, but he didn't say anything."

"Aye, Martin's one of the good ones," observed Bobe Elka with a wry smile. "So you nicked a clavis, eh? Kurra?"

Kurra materialised, as it were, in front of Chi.

Chi let out a squeak of alarm. "Honestly, I wish you'd give me a warning when you were going to do that!"

Kurra turned to face the company, so as to address Chi and Bobe Elka. "It were not just the abbey clavis that I took," she started, and held up her hand, twisted something in the empty space before her. The air shimmered, misted. Chi's eyes went wobbly. And there was another clavis, clutched in Kurra's large, hairy hand, firelight glinting from its bronze vertices.

"Hoho!" exclaimed Bobe Elka. "This hob is a sly one, Chi, do you not think? So the Witcerce gateway is closed for good, with you havin' both keys?" She cackled, long and hard. "Reckon as the Ostiarium ain't goin' to be too pleased with that!"

"I do not intend to tell them," stated Kurra. "I do not trust Aelene. And it was necessary to prevent Martin from opening the gateway to allow Aedredd to pursue us. Should he have been minded to."

"Which, to be fair, he didn't try to do," Chi reminded the hob.

"Dinner's ready!" announced Shireen, who had been busy at the fire, tending a large steaming iron pan. "It's Tahdig. King Cyrus's favourite." She hefted the pan and tipped it out onto a tray, a huge mound of bright yellow rice with a baked crispy topping. It steamed in the evening chill. The smell, saffron and turmeric, redolent of Araby, had Chidiebere salivating.

"Here you are, duck. Spare plate." Bobe Elka passed a plate and fork to Chi, who grinned thanks to her. "An' there's some milk, of sorts, 'ere, if you prefer, hob." She passed a sealed container of heat-treated, long-life milk to Kurra, whose eyes glowed with thanks and pleasure in equal measure.

CHI FINISHED THE LAST of the burnt crust of rice that was stuck to the bottom of the pan. Somehow, the caramelisation of this layer made it even tastier than the main portion she had eaten. Shireen smiled over at her, eyes glinting in the firelight like amber jewels. She almost chuckled as Chi attacked the pan with a metal spoon.

"It is one of the most delicious dishes. Tricky, on a fire. I am getting used to it, now." Her accent was heavy, Persian or one of the desert states, Chi thought.

"Have you been on the road for long?"

"I have been living like this for ..." She paused, looked up at the sky, lost in memory. "For six years. It is not so long. I have been fortunate to have George as a friend. He has shown me the ropes."

"Wow. Six years. I've not been out of school six years!"

"You will soon find that time flies by. This world, though ... it is something, no?" She gestured with her arm, bracelets jangling as she moved.

"I've only been here a day. It's taking some getting used to." Chi held up her phone. "No signal."

"Yes, there is nothing electrical here. I like it like that."

With no preamble, Ailesh the dog sat bolt upright from her supine position by the fire, hackles raised, letting out a low growl; she was facing the road towards Witcerce and Wayland.

Kurra appeared in front of Chi.

"Chidiebere-ma'am," she whispered, "Aedredd is almost upon us! We must flee!"

Kurra's face was a mask of worry and fear. George got up from his box where he had been rolling a cigarette and took up a quarterstaff from where it rested against the front of his wagon. He strode away into the dark, with Ailesh at his heels still growling, the sound low and deep.

"We'll be away into the Betwixt, I reckons," said Bobe Elka, walking up to Chi.

"B-betwixt?" It was all too fast! Raised voices came from down the road from where George had gone. Barks and shouts.

"I will assist George. And flee to the woods if necessary. Good luck, Chidiebere-ma'am," Kurra said, giving Chi's leg a brief pat as she ran past, heading towards the shouting and barking. Chi looked after the hob, whose diminutive form faded into the gloom. She looked back at the fire. Shireen had put down the last plate she was washing up and was reaching for a large, curved sword in a scabbard, that was resting, unnoticed, in the arc of her vardo's front.

"I too will assist George. We are used to skirmishes, Chi, do not worry." She gave a grim smile, a wave of her bangled arm and melted into the dark after Kurra, silent as an owl.

"Now, lass. Best not to tarry. Here, like Josephine showed you, you think the spell and walk to the mist, I'll see you in there, like. These are the words: 'Sikker sa yogs, lasta sa yogs.'" A mist sprang up, literally rising from the ground, enveloping the fire. "Think them words, walk into the mist, I'll be along in a second. Off you go!" She gave Chi a gentle shove in the small of her back. Chi grabbed her bag, shuffled towards the fire. The mist was icy cold, her breath condensing in clouds before her face.

Reality turned its back for a moment and Chi found herself in a monotonic world of grey. The fire seemed to shrink to nothing more than a pinprick of flickering yellow light. Bobe Elka arrived as if moving at an incredible speed, and stood, leaning on her staff, beads of water in her hair and on her cloak.

"Welcome to the Betwixt. Come on, we can get to Mediolanum in a few steps."

"But ... where are we? And what about Kurra, the others?"

"We're between here and there. Betwixt. It works on yogs." Seeing her confused expression, Bobe Elka explained, "Yog. It's Romani for fire. Betwixt spell works on campfires. Takes you from one to another. Handy, like. Come on, your hob will be fine. She's been around long enough. An' George is old-school. I've no worries about him. Not with Shireen around, anyways." Bobe Elka walked a few steps and peered at the floor. There was another tiny yellow pinprick of light on the misty grey ground. "This will do us. Hearth in Mediolanum. Findir the baker. One of us, sort of. Have a look. Say the other half of the spell, and step into the image."

Chidiebere did as she was told, looked into the pinprick of light, which somehow resolved into an aerial view of a baker's shop; a rotund being, the presumed Findir, was loading dough-filled trays into a huge oven, the light of the fire casting flickers on his face.

"The other 'alf is this: 'kathal yog, adala yog,'" said Bobe Elka. As Chi thought the spell, she felt the pull of the magic, then a blast of heat and, stumbling, reached out to steady herself on a table laden with bread tins, each one filled with dough ready for the oven. One tin fell to the floor with a clatter.

"Great Goddess!" came the baker's baritone exclamation, as he turned at the noise. He was perhaps four feet tall and had an enormous red beard, a round face and piercing eyes. "Who are you? Where did you spring from? You can't just materialise in my bakery without so much as knocking!" Chi started to speak but then felt the pressure change in the air as Bobe Elka appeared beside her.

"Ah! Elka! Good. I was hoping to have a word!" his voice boomed.

Chapter 18

"Stand aside. Who are you to block my path? Do you not know who I am?" The sibilant hiss of Aedredd's speech reached Kurra as she rushed to join George and Ailesh at the corner of the road. She had spotted Aedredd's four-wheel-drive truck approaching, a minute earlier, from the same corner. An elven glamour washed about the ether; a powerful coercion. George didn't seem bothered by it. When she arrived at his side, he was leaning on his quarterstaff, standing before the truck, silhouetted by the glare of its yellowing headlamps. Aedredd was standing by the open door of the truck.

"Aye, I know you. Your glamour won't do nowt 'ere. But I reckon as you're after the black girl? She's gone," said George, his voice low and dangerous.

"I am after that thieving, spying hobgoblin," she replied, pointing at Kurra. "She has stolen claves from Witcerce."

"Funny," countered George, still leaning on his staff. "Didn't realise you worked for the Ostiarium."

Intense fury flooded Aedredd's face. This, Kurra mused, did not look like it would end well. As she was thinking this, Shireen arrived, moving with grace and silence, like a cat.

She unsheathed a curved sword from its scabbard, the edge glinting in the vehicle's lights. "We will see the claves returned to their rightful owner," she said. "Leave this place in peace. That way." Shireen pointed with her sword, down the road from which Aedredd had approached. Away from the wagons. The sword made a noise as it moved through the air, as if it were singing a keening note.

Aedredd turned towards the vehicle's open door. She gestured to the occupant, and the far door opened. The soldier from the factory stepped out, hefting a stubby modern musket. He took aim at the trio from behind the door.

"Shoot them all," said Aedredd, ice in her voice.

Kurra instantly started moving, pushing into slow time. The soldier and George and Ailesh froze in place, but to Kurra's astonishment, Aedredd and Shireen were moving almost as fast as she was. She could feel Aedredd's magic pulling at her own slow time, feeding from it.

Shireen had morphed into a glowing, orange-ochre-coloured being, leaving behind a sparkling trail of amber motes glittering in her wake as she powered towards the soldier, dirt cascading backwards from her feet. The soldier was halfway through drawing the bolt back to make the weapon ready as she raised her sword and sliced at the door, the rifle. The blade passed through the barrel and mechanism of the gun, which flew upwards in two pieces, fingers from the soldier's left hand also flying away, arcs of blood glittering in the headlights.

Aedredd raised her hand and threw an indistinct ball of energy, or enchantment, at Kurra. It distorted the air between them, moving at an incredible speed, making a fluting noise as it powered towards Kurra. She tried to duck out of the way but didn't have time to move far, and was caught with a glancing blow. It was like being hit by an invisible giant's hand. She was lifted bodily from the ground and flung backwards, towards the edge of the forest. She landed in a rolling heap, smashing through ferns and loam, dropping from slow time with a thump.

She looked up from her prone position in the ferns. George was raising his staff, stepping forward. Ailesh launched herself at the soldier, clamping her jaws onto his leg below the remains of the vehicle door. But Kurra could see the man was a spent force, clutching his bleeding hand, alternately whimpering and screaming. Kurra looked at Aedredd. She was standing exactly where she had been, a sneer distorting her face. There was a healing wound on her forehead, a jagged cut, with what looked like stitches.

"Ailesh, leave 'im," George commanded, and Ailesh released the soldier's leg from her jaws, allowing the man to collapse fully on the ground where he continued to utter profanities in Calabrian.

Shireen returned to George's side, flickering into existence from her own version of slow time, her sword held high, over one shoulder, pointed at Aedredd. An afterimage of amber sparks flickered about her. The vehicle's four tyres were all slashed, and it settled onto the wheel rims with a sigh.

"I am impressed," hissed Aedredd. "I did not know there were any djinn yet residing in the world. However, the fact remains that the hobgoblin has stolen from me. Spied on me. Aligned herself against the true rulers of Khôra. So. My turn." She threw her hands before her, and the ground in front of George and Shireen exploded upwards, stones and mud and sod flying into their faces. They fell back with shouts of pain.

Kurra couldn't ask them to continue this. She knew how powerful and deranged Aedredd was.

"Catch me if you can," she rasped, scrambling into the woods on the far side of the road, pushing into slow time once more. It worked, and she pushed hard. Maybe she was lucky and Aedredd was drawing breath before casting her slow time net. Maybe Kurra had already put enough distance between them. It didn't matter. What mattered was that she had managed to get into slow time and start moving as fast as she could away from the combatants; hoping to draw Aedredd away.

Elvish glamour writhed in the ether behind her. The slow time enchantments employed by Aedredd tried to tangle her legs. One of the warbling, fluting balls of energy seared the air above her head, hit a tree, the trunk exploding in a shower of splinters and chunks of wood, bark. Kurra ducked below the flying debris. Kept running, zigzagging through the trees, barely able to see anything in the dim light from the just-rising moon. She heard crashing and cursing behind her. Aedredd was following her, that much was obvious. Good.

Kurra burst into a clearing in the forest. Relief surged through her. For a moment she had thought she'd taken off in the wrong direction, would miss it altogether. She hared across the clearing, leapt over the centre and skidded to a halt at the far tree line.

Aedredd emerged from the understorey on the opposite side of the clearing, not fifty yards away. Kurra stepped back into real time. Aedredd's magic disengaged, and she stumbled as she also fell back into real time.

"You!" she spat. "You are going to die. You have made a fool of me, have stolen from me!" She sprinted across the glade, heading straight for Kurra.

Oh, I really hope this works, thought Kurra, offering a silent prayer to ... Hestia? She didn't know. Time to re-engage with the gods, she supposed. Especially if this worked.

As Aedredd reached the centre of the clearing she stumbled, yelled an obscenity, flailed her arms, and disappeared downwards. There was a dull thud and another shriek. Kurra let out a ragged breath she hadn't realised she was holding.

"Now then, gang, looks like we've caught ourselves an elf, an' a high an' mighty one, at that!" came the jovial voice of Kaelith, as he swaggered out of the tree line next to Kurra. "Good job leading her in like that, Kurra. Come on, let's go have a look-see, eh?"

Kurra followed the hob, Kaelith, to the edge of the pit trap in the centre of the clearing. A handful of other hobs appeared from the trees, all dressed in tatty, much-patched forest-green and brown. They wore pheasant feathers woven into their long hair and were barefoot like all hobs but with bows and arrows, knives, tiny swords. A regular woodland army, Kurra thought. Khôra's own resistance.

Epilogue

Look at you, destitute in the woods. Pathetic ...

"Thou canst not hurt me no more. Thou art not real. I be happy. An' I be free. Thou art jealous. So, shu' up," Kurra told her whining voice. Its interruptions to Kurra's days had become less and less frequent. Kurra was confident that eventually, it would be silent forever.

She stretched out on the loam floor and looked up at the treetops, which were swaying in a gentle breeze. Stands of hazel and silver birch, their leaves fluttering, like tiny paper bells. The thinnest branches stretched skyward, whispering and murmuring the story of the forest.

She could sense someone coming through the Betwixt, that cold space that she had once thought of as just her own realm. A mist formed around the campfire, rising as if from the very ground. A green-cloaked figure materialised through the fog, tendrils of dew trailing in the air behind her.

"Bobe Elka. Kushti divvus." Kurra, sitting up, greeted the old hedge witch, who put her hood down and shook out her white hair. Kurra reached for a spare cup and put the small, blackened kettle back to boil on the tiny fire.

"Kushti divvus, yersen, Kurra. Well met. How you keepin'?"

"I am well, thank thee. Tea?"

"Not that awful stuff you made from polecat piss and alder tree bark?"

Kurra smiled. Her experiments in tea brewing from the wildwood had become the talk of the area. "I do have some teabags from Defaltum Mundi; I think they might even hail from Breotonlond."

"Well, that would be a treat. And, I brought you a parcel of stuff, like. Maybe there's summat in there you could try, an' all."

Kurra's ears pricked up at this news. A parcel! Intriguing. "Are you now a delivery service, Bobe, travelling gently by campfire?"

The old lady laughed. "Nay, lass. This is a special delivery, like. Here you go." She reached into her travel knapsack and pulled out a package wrapped in brown paper and tied with hessian string. She handed it to Kurra, who hefted it. It was almost as big as she was! "Tis from Chidiebere the Plumber Sorcerer. As if you couldn't guess." She was smiling.

Kurra's heart leapt, and she set the parcel on the ground, pulled at the string. She unwrapped the paper to reveal eight tins of condensed milk. And a tin-opener device. And a letter, sealed with a wax stamp. Whilst her heart and stomach were fluttering their excitement at the concept of so much concentrated milk goodness, she reached first for the letter. The wax seal held the image of a spanner and a droplet of water, with a hexagonal motif behind it. Plumber sorcerer. She smiled. Slid a hairy finger under the flap and ripped the envelope open. The letter was written in cursive, and Kurra had to concentrate hard to decipher it. Chidiebere's handwriting was awful, she decided.

Bolerum, September 23rd.

My dear Kurra,

I do hope this letter finds you well. It's weird writing to you, rather than texting or emailing like I would anyone else. But not so weird, really. I am back and forth every now and then to Khôra through the Bolerum gateway in the west. I moved out of Witcerce. I felt being away from the factory and the Gratadei would be a good idea. I'm sure you know what I mean.

I'm based way down in the southwest, now. I like it. The sea is amazing. And I'm doing a lot of plumbing. I learnt some more spells from Josephine (who says hello, by the way!) so I'm sort of in and out of Khôra doing plumbing jobs there too. And a bit of work on the side for the Ostiarium.

The pumps were, as I'm sure you know, built despite our efforts, and delivered via the Mediolanum gateway. They had to move them on huge lorries from Witcerce through all of Europa to Milano to get them to a gateway that was big enough. So we did some good, I suppose. No one knows what the pumps are pumping, but this is the Gratadei, so, nothing good, right?

And *the Gratadei have now taken over the Mediolanum gateway and most of the others, apart from Bolerum and I think the one on Ninguaria (what you will know as Erytheia). So it looks like Khôra will be isolated, soon. I can't risk being stuck there with Aedredd still on the loose, so ... I do hope you'll be OK. I think of you all the time.*

Speaking of Aedredd, I heard from George and Shireen (who, it turns out, is a djinn, but I suppose you knew that?!) That you enlisted the help of the Partigiani? How on earth? I suppose slow time, and they are hobs as well ... Please write and tell me, I'm fascinated! It's a shame they had to let Aedredd go, but I suppose random killings of high-born elves are frowned upon ...

*I hope the tins of condensed milk are OK? Mam said they would be useful for you for emergency eye-googling! Oh, and she says you are welcome any time at her house as you are the nicest hob she's ever met! I didn't know she knew **any** hobs, but there you go!*

I hope to meet up with you again someday, but it looks like things will get worse before they get better. Keep hiding in the woods, Kurra! Bobe Elka said she can find you, and she's the best hedge witch I know, so I'm sure she will, but I hope you stay hidden from Aedredd and THEM!

Sending thoughts and lots of love,
~ Chidiebere-ma'am the Plumber Sorcerer. Xx

- End -

About the Author

Adam is an author of fantasy novels and historical fiction-non-fiction novels.

When he's not inventing stuff or wiring things up, he's writing, or out and about on his horse, exploring the hidden byeways and the deeper wooded sections of the Peak District.

Sign up to the newsletter for future publishing dates, news, cover reveals and free e-books from the website.

Read more at https://www.adamfoxauthor.co.uk.

About the Publisher

Foxes' Retreat is a writer's haven in the heart of the Peak District in England.

Read more on their website.

Read more at https://www.foxesretreat.com.